An U

Steve Bellinger

Wordwooze Publishing

wordwooze.com

There's no fiction like science fiction

Steve Bellinger

DEDICATION & ACKNOWLEDGEMENTS

For my Mom, Dorothy Bellinger, who taught me how to appreciate a good
book
- and -
For my daughter Annika, my biggest fan

A few years ago my dear wife Donna, an author in her own right (*You
Lost Me @ Hello, Actionable Principles That Move You Beyond Networking*),
picked up an early draft of *The Chronocar* and after reading it, threatened to
divorce me if I did not finish it. Thank you, sweetheart.

One of the best things you can do as a writer is surround yourself with
other writers. I joined a MeetUp group called "Just Write" where you spend
an hour or so writing, then another hour socializing and discussing your
projects. It took a year of these weekly meetings to finally finish *The
Chronocar*. Then I bit the bullet and sought out critique groups, where other
writers would read and offer constructive criticism and suggestions. I actually
tried several.

The most helpful one was the Monday Night Edgewater Writers Group.
A special thanks to Rick Anton and James Tajiri (who stuck with me through
two groups), the founder Susan Bass, Nicole Braun, and Sonja Foxe.

TABLE OF CONTENTS

Chapter 1 1

Chapter 2 11

Chapter 3 19

Chapter 4 33

Chapter 5 39

Chapter 6 46

Chapter 7 59

Chapter 8 61

Chapter 9 67

Chapter 10 81

Chapter 11 87

Chapter 12 89

Chapter 13 90

Chapter 14 97

Chapter 15 100

Chapter 16 104

Chapter 17 111

Biography 123

Chapter 1

August 11, 1888

Somewhere near Jackson, Mississippi

Straw Boss called out "Quittin' time!" just before the whistle blew. Thirty shirtless exhausted men, their brawny bodies gleaming with sweat in the hot Mississippi sun, stopped what they were doing, not wanting to give the company a minute more than what they were getting paid for. It was a typical railroad work gang: coolies from China carried and placed the heavy ties, their bowed heads covered in traditional straw hats, and the Irishmen were trusted with actually laying the track. But the Negro men did the hardest and dirtiest work—digging ditches, moving big rocks, and some were allowed to pound in the spikes that fastened the iron to the wooden ties. Three and a half miles of fresh railroad track lay behind them, and nobody had died. It had been a good day.

Simmie Johnson was in mid-swing. His herculean arms glistened in the sun as he brought the big hammer down. His cousin Willie held the stake in place and barely got his hand away as Simmie punched it several inches into the ground with a loud *plink*! Only one more stroke to go.

Simmie wielded the heavy mallet with ease. He was a tall, buff, handsome young black man with a gentle nature about him, qualities that did not go unnoticed by young females. But Simmie had no time for women. Not now, at least. He had more important things to concern himself with, like finishing up here, collecting his pay, and getting home. The time would soon come when he would leave this dreadful life behind and make something of himself. Soon, very soon.

"Come on, Simmie," Willie called. "We done fo' today."

Simmie followed Willie and the other weary workers to the tool wagon, where they surrendered their picks, shovels, and hammers to Straw Boss, a wiry, middle-aged, sunburned white man who had earned his position solely through his heritage.

"Put mine in the corner," Willie said as he handed in his pick. "I want to use the same one next week." Straw Boss threw Willie's pick onto the pile.

"Hurry up, Simmie." Willie tugged his arm as Simmie lifted the heavy hammer to Straw Boss, who almost toppled out of the wagon from the weight. A minute later they were standing in line at the pay wagon where Old Mr. Sykes distributed the wages.

Sykes was a chubby old man who wore thick spectacles and a green eyeshade that framed his balding head. "Okay, Willie J." Sykes adjusted his glasses and licked his thumb. Then he peeled off dollar bills and counted out coins as he read off Willie's pay record. "Five dollars and seventy-five cents."

"Thank ya, suh." Willie bowed, which was a slight gesture, since his back naturally bent forward.

"Simmie Johnson," Sykes said as he flipped through the book. Simmie stepped forward. "Here you go—seven dollars and twenty-five cents."

"Thank you," Simmie said, wondering why he should thank the man for giving him the money he had worked so hard to earn.

"Wait!" Willie grabbed Simmie's arm and glared at Sykes. "Why he get more than me?"

"You didn't show up for work on Wednesday," Sykes said flatly, "and you left early yesterday. Lucky I don't fire you!"

Willie frowned. "White man tryin' to cheat me," he mumbled as they stepped out of line.

"He's not trying to cheat you." Simmie sighed. "You've got to work a full day to get a full day's pay."

"You as bad as him," Willie said, stuffing the money into his pocket. "Come on, let's go get somethin' to drink."

Simmie carefully folded his money, placed it in a tattered envelope, and slipped it into his pocket. "I told you before, I don't drink, and I don't carouse around."

"Naw, man, I mean let's go to Ol' Ben's and get a cold pop."

Simmie saw no harm in that, so they started down the dusty road toward town. Willie talked Black Pete into joining them. Black Pete was big, dark-skinned, and had even less sense than Willie. Simmie walked a few paces ahead of them, lost in thought.

"The quantity of motion, which is collected by taking the sum of the motions directed towards the same parts, and the difference of those that are directed to contrary parts, suffers no change from the action of bodies among themselves."

"Hey, Simmie!"

"What?" Simmie said, annoyed at the interruption.

"How come it is that you so smart?" Willie asked.

"What?"

"I mean, you can read, you can do 'cipherin'. You about as smart as any white man."

Simmie stopped and looked at him. "Maybe smarter."

"But why?" Willie said.

"Yeah, why?" Black Pete parroted.

Simmie shrugged. "I guess the good Lord saw fit to bless me with a good mind."

"But why?" Willie asked again.

"I don't know. Ask him." Simmie pointed toward the sky as he started walking again.

"Don't make no sense," Willie puzzled. "Why would the Lord give them kinds of smarts to a colored man?"

"What in the hell are you talking about, Willie?" Simmie stopped walking again.

"You smart, Simmie. Smarter than all the white men we works for. But what can you do with it?"

Simmie turned and resumed his pace. "I got plans." He put his hand in his pocket and felt the envelope with money inside. Just a little more money and he could get away from this place. Then, finally, he could put his mind to work. No more pretending to be stupid just to stay out of trouble with the white man.

"What kind of plans?" Willie asked.

"I got plans. Don't you worry about what kind. They are my plans. Hopefully, it is God's will that I see them through."

"So, you do believe they's a God, right?"

"Now, what kind of question is that?" Simmie scowled. "*I'm* the one who has to read the scriptures to *you* every night."

"Big Momma say you don't believe. Big Momma say you a heathen!"

"A heathen!" Black Pete echoed.

"Big Momma," Simmie scoffed. "What does she know?"

"She say you study the devil," Willie said softly.

"The devil," Black Pete whispered.

"Now, why would she say that?"

"'Cause she found that book under yo' bed."

Simmie turned and faced Willie. "What book?" he asked, knowing full well which book. He only owned two. And what was Big Momma doing going through his things?

"That… prince book." Willie cringed under Simmie's glare.

"*The Principia?* She found my *Principia?*" he asked, carefully using the pronunciation that Miss Abigail had taught him six years ago.

Willie looked around to make sure no one could hear him. "She said all the crazy writin' and the lines and circles and numbers was all the work of the

3

devil!"

"Man, what you been doin'?" Black Pete cried.

"Big Momma don't know… What did she do with my book?" Simmie snatched Willie by the collar. "What did she do with my book?"

"Sh-she burned it," Willie said meekly.

"Good thang!" Black Pete said.

"Shut up, Pete!" Simmie bellowed, and Black Pete cowered away. "She burned my book?" He imagined his prize possession aflame. One of the most important things he owned, the thing that sparked his dream of starting a new life. He felt a tightening in his gut.

"She said it was the work of the devil and that it was goin' to ruin yo' soul. She burned it to protect you, to keep you and all the rest of us from goin' to hell!"

"She burned my book?" Simmie roared as he raised a fist.

"Don't hit me! I didn't do it!" Willie cried. "Big Momma did!"

Simmie released Willie and tried to calm himself. His *Principia*! He had had that book since he was twelve years old when he rescued it from the trash behind the town library. So what if the pages were tattered and the cover was torn off? It was *his* book! He had begged Miss Abigail, the teacher at the white children's school, to teach him to read, just so he could discover what that book was all about. After he'd breezed his way through all of the readers and textbooks she had, he showed her his *Principia*. She'd looked at it and dismissed it as nonsense, which Simmie found to be odd since she had heard of it and even knew the correct pronunciation of the title. It turned out that she had never actually seen a copy of it before, and young Simmie was able to understand it all better than she could. And the knowledge! The wisdom! Written two hundred years ago by Sir Isaac Newton, a genius of a man! It was as valuable to Simmie as his Bible. For over six years he coveted that book, and now Big Momma, in her senile ignorance, had destroyed it. Fortunately, Simmie had it all memorized.

"What about the rest of my stuff?" Simmie growled.

"I-I don't know. All I saw was the book." Willie kept out of reach. "Simmie?"

"Don't talk to me," Simmie grumbled, and walked ahead. Was it Big Momma's fault that she did not understand? She was only doing what she thought was best for her family. After all, it was she who had had the courage to rescue baby Simmie when his parents were sold off and he was left to die because he was sickly and of no practical value. When he got older, she'd also recognized that there was something special about him, that he was a lot

4

smarter than all the other kids, black or white. She had taught him to hide his smarts lest he offend some white person.

He looked over his shoulder and noticed that Black Pete had fallen behind, walking slowly with a blank expression on his face. "Come here, Pete."

Obediently, Black Pete ran up to Simmie. "What you want?"

Simmie sighed. "Sorry I hollered at you."

"That's okay. Everybody does." Black Pete grinned.

Simmie sadly looked at Black Pete. He used to have good sense just like everybody else until he'd accidentally been hit on the head with a shovel a year ago. The good Lord saw fit to give Simmie a good mind, and he took Black Pete's mind away from him.

"I won't holler at you again, Pete."

"Okay, Simmie."

Simmie wondered if Black Pete realized that he was slow in the head or if the Lord had been kind enough to hide that fact from him. Well, there was nothing Simmie could do now except try to look out for him. He gave Black Pete a pat on the back of the head and walked on. Soon he was again lost in thought. Recalling details from his beloved *Principia* made dealing with this terrible world a little less painful.

"If bodies, any how moved among themselves, are urged in the direction of parallel lines by equal accelerative forces, they will all continue to move among themselves, after the same manner as if they had been urged by no such forces."

It was twilight when they entered the little town with its dilapidated wooden buildings and dirt path. Only a couple of men were sitting on the porch of the saloon on the side of the road. The General Store, an old house of gray weathered wood, sat in the middle of it all. The upstairs windows were boarded up. A couple of rocking chairs sat on the porch, and rusty metal signs advertising cigarettes, booze, and soft drinks hung on the outside. They walked up the steps, and the proprietor, a short, wrinkly, old white man with a scraggly beard, came out and met them at the door.

"You know you boys can't come in here," Old Ben said, chewing on a corncob pipe.

"We just want some cold pop," Willie said.

"All a-ya's?"

"Yes, suh," Willie bowed.

"Okay, three grape pops. Wait here." Old Ben disappeared inside.

"I don't likes grape," Black Pete protested. "I likes orange!"

5

"White man think all we like is grape pop, then grape pop is what you gets," Willie admonished.

"Okay, Willie," Black Pete said.

Simmie shook his head and sighed when Black Pete and Willie performed like cowering coons in front of this dim-witted old white man. It was going to be up to Simmie to get out of this stinking hole and make something of himself so black people could hold their heads high in the future. Well, *his* descendants, at least.

Old Ben came back out with three sweaty bottles of purple liquid. "That'll be six cents."

"The sign says a penny a bottle," Simmie said flatly.

"Six cents," Old Ben repeated.

Simmie gave the old man six pennies. It took a moment for Old Ben to count the money.

"All right. Now, you boys go 'round back to drink that, ya hear?"

"Yes, suh." Willie bowed again.

Old Ben went back inside while Willie and Black Pete made their way behind the store. Simmie gazed at the darkening sky. While other men dreamed of freedom or wealth, Simmie dreamed of stars and planets, and of time and space, and how it all worked according to Mr. Newton. The full moon was high, surrounded by a sprinkling of tiny lights. One very bright star was just a little to the left, the brightest one in the sky. Simmie knew it wasn't a star. It was the planet Venus, orbiting around the sun, just like Earth.

"That Mercury and Venus revolve about the sun is evident from their moon-like appearances. When they shine out with a full face, they are, in respect of us, beyond or above the sun; when they appear half full, they are about the same height on one side or other of the sun; when horned, they are below or between us and the sun; and they are sometimes, when directly under, like spots traversing the sun's disk."

He took a sip from his bottle. Amazing—the planets, the Earth, all revolving around the sun, thanks to an almost-magical thing called gravity.

"The planets move in ellipses which have their common focus in the centre of the sun; and, by radii drawn to that centre…"

"Boy! What the hell you think you doin'?"

"Uh, what?" Simmie looked down to see Old Ben's scowling face.

"I told you to drink that 'round back! You think you can do what you want to around here, nigger?" He slapped the bottle from Simmie's hand, and it rolled down the dirt road, leaving a trail of foamy liquid.

"I'm sorry, I'm sorry." Simmie, a giant of a man compared to Old Ben,

6

backed away. "I'll just leave, all right?"

"What's goin' on over there, Ben?" A young white man stepped out of the saloon and crossed the road.

"He told me to drink my pop around back, but I forgot. I started drinking it here. I made a mistake. I'm sorry." Simmie said as he glanced over at Willie and Black Pete, who were peeking around the corner of the building. Terror shone in their eyes.

"Ain't nobody talkin' to you, boy! You shut your nigger mouth," the man said.

"He disrespected me, Jed," Old Ben said. "Was gonna hit me, too."

"That's not true!" Simmie protested.

"You callin' Ol' Ben a liar?" Jed growled. "You just one smart-assed nigger, ain't cha? I'm just gonna have to teach you a lesson!" Jed unbuckled his belt and yanked it out from his belt loops. "Now, you take yo' pants down, and I'm gonna give you a whippin' you ain't never gonna forget."

Simmie's head was spinning. Willie and Black Pete were long gone. Other white men looked out of windows and peeked out of doorways. *Just accept the humiliation and take the whipping,* he reasoned, but he knew it would not end there. Simmie was bigger and stronger than Jed and could probably handle two or even three men like him, but he knew if he was not very careful, he would be hanging from a tree somewhere in the woods before the night was over. He needed to think fast.

"I said take your pants down, boy!" Jed reached over and pulled at Simmie's pants.

"To every action there is always opposed an equal reaction…"

Simmie planted a huge fist in Jed's face. Blood splattered. Jed fell to the ground and lay motionless.

Old Ben shrieked, "You killed him! You murderin' nigger! You done killed Jed!"

"Just knocked him out," Simmie said quietly. "He'll be okay."

"He killed him! Damned nigger done killed Jed!" Old Ben yelled.

Several men were now on the street, trying to make out what was going on in the moonlight. Old Ben was bent over Jed, crying and screaming. Simmie took off and ran.

This was every Negro man's worst nightmare and one Simmie had lived with every day. It was damned near impossible for a black man to not get into trouble. It had been 23 years since the war had ended, and his people were supposed to be free. But the South was still a very dangerous place for a black man. He had managed to avoid problems up until now, staying to himself, and prudently taking the insults and abuse when they came. Another month or so and he would have been free of all this.

Simmie ran as hard as he could, his legs and arms aching from a full day of backbreaking work. For several hours he hid in the dark woods, concealing himself in trees and bushes, playing hide-and-seek with the lynch mobs. Around midnight he found himself on a ridge overlooking the shantytown he had called home. Some white men were going door to door, bursting into the ramshackle houses, sometimes dragging some poor soul outside, beating the hell out of him, and carrying him off. Simmie watched, torn between reveling in the good fortune of having escaped the violence and feeling badly for those who had not. Later, long after the last of the posse was gone, he made his way home.

"Oh, Lord, it's Simmie." Willie looked terrified when he cracked open the door.

"Give him his mess and send him off," Big Momma said. She was a slight, wrinkled, dark-skinned old woman in a dingy white dress. Simmie saw her sitting in the corner, waving her frail fist in the air. "Don't let that heathen back in this house!"

Willie pushed a burlap sack through the half-open door. "You know they got poor ol' Black Pete. They beat him somethin' awful and took him. Probably hangin' from some tree branch by now."

"They got Black Pete?" Simmie said as he swallowed a lump in his throat. He looked in the bag, which contained all the clothes he had in the world as well as his Bible, pencil, notebook, and a small box of matches.

"Poor boy dead 'cause a you!" Big Momma called from inside. "Go on before ya get us all kilt!"

"Bye, Simmie," Willie said sheepishly as he closed the door.

Simmie felt guilty about Black Pete, but there was nothing he could do for him; he was with the Lord now.

Maybe Black Pete was the lucky one.

Simmie went around to the back of the house and paced 50 feet into the woods. Using one of the half-dozen matches, he located the spot in the dirt, dug up the old whiskey bottle that contained his savings, and broke it against a rock. When he added his wages for the week, the total amounted to $63.37, more than enough to get him where he wanted to go. Twenty minutes later, he was deep in the woods again, guided by the light of the full moon. His plan was to get to the train yard, hop a freight, and when he was far enough away, purchase a proper train ticket.

Cold and exhausted after 11 hours of slinging a hammer and moving heavy boulders, he was in no condition to be on the run. He wanted to stop, start a fire, warm up, and rest for a few minutes. He heard barking in the distance. *Dogs! Damn! They never give up!* He risked lighting a match for a second to check his compass, then headed east.

When he reached the stream, he stripped naked and tossed his clothes as high as he could into the trees. He washed himself in the chilly water and put on a clean shirt and pants from his bag. He soaked his shoes before putting them back on. It was going to be uncomfortable, but he hoped it would throw the dogs off his scent.

On the other side of the stream, he walked another half mile or so, where he found a large tree with gigantic branches that would make a nice cradle. He climbed up and made himself as comfortable as possible, nearly 20 feet above the ground. Damp and shivering, he used his bag as a pillow and settled in for the night, not daring to sleep for fear he would either not hear the approach of a lynch mob or fall out of the tree.

"The force of gravity, considered downward from the surface of the planets decreases nearly in the proportion of the distances from their centres. If the matter of the planet were of an uniform density, this Proposition would be accurately true."

Stars winked in and out as leaves above fluttered in the wind. *How far away could those stars be?* he thought. *Is there even a number that can describe the distance? The absolute wonder of God's creation, so beautiful and so precise. Beyond belief, but not beyond understanding. From the planets and stars in the sky to the leaves on the trees, men can understand.* Simmie felt that he could understand if he had had the chance to read more and to learn. There had to be so much more than in the *Principia*. How much more knowledge had been acquired in the two centuries since Mr. Newton?

Perhaps he would still get that chance if he could get the hell out of Jackson alive. So long had he saved his money and planned. Just a few more days and he would have left anyway. If only he had not been forced to punch that white man. Maybe he should have just swallowed his pride this time and bowed and shuffled like a good nigger. If only he had gone around the back of the store with Willie and Black Pete. If only he had just gone straight home after work like he usually did. He'd be sleeping in his warm bed now instead of perched—cowering, wet, and cold—in a tree. Black Pete would be still alive, too.

"Absolute, true, and mathematical time, of itself, and from its own nature flows equably without regard to anything external, and by another name is called duration…"

What if he could go back? Back to the time before the encounter with Old Ben and Jed? The choice to go for the fateful bottle of pop was like a fork in the road. That simple choice had completely changed the course of his life. Was it possible to go back to that fork? Was there some way he could go back, knowing which choice was best, and forgo the cold drink for the safety of home? Was that somehow possible?

Off in the distance, he heard a dog howling. Simmie lay quietly as the baying got louder. They could not have possibly followed him here, could they?

"Come on, Peps." Simmie heard a man talking to his hound. "I know you smell him! You got him, don't ya?"

Simmie trembled when the dog ran up to his tree, barking wildly.

"Yeah! You got him, Peps!" The man yanked the dog back and yelled up to the tree, "You up there, nigger? Might as well come on down if you is!"

Simmie held his breath. Was this it? Was this the end?

"All right, boy! I gave ya a chance. I get just as much for ya dead as alive."

Simmie heard him cock the rifle. He closed his eyes and tensed his muscles. "Lord, thy will be done," he prayed to himself, waiting for the sting of the bullet.

Bang!

There was a rustle in the tree above. Something fell on Simmie's chest. Startled, he brushed it off and heard it fall to the ground.

"The hell is this? Peps, it's a damned squirrel! You stupid, biscuit-eatin' bitch! We ain't out to get no damn squirrels!"

Peps went wild, yelping and trying to climb the tree.

"Get back here, ya good for nothin'." The dog squealed as the man yanked him by the rope around its neck. "Gonna pay a lot of money for that nigger's ass, and you goddamn chasin' squirrels? Come on!"

The yelling and barking grew softer as Simmie watched the bouncing light of the man's lantern disappear into the woods. The gnarled tree branches held him securely as he glanced up at the starry night one last time before falling asleep.

Chapter 2

Sunlight shafted through the leaves and burned through his eyelids. How long had he slept? Simmie shifted in his tree bed. His clothes were dry, but his shirt was still sticky with the blood of the dead squirrel. Something was wrong. There was nothing under his head. The sack containing all of his worldly possessions was gone! He climbed down to a lower branch and jumped to the ground. Simmie let out a sigh of relief when he found it lying on the ground; some of its contents had spilled out onto the dirt.

His back and arms ached. His stomach growled. His legs were sore. But it was time to get moving. He dug his compass out of the sack; the glass was cracked, but it still worked. The train yard should be a couple of miles northwest. Gathering up his things, he threw the bag over his shoulder and started walking.

What would the coming days, weeks, and months have in store? If it were possible to look into the future, could it be changed? He definitely had plans—carefully thought-out plans. But there were so many things beyond his control. What if he didn't have enough money? What if he wasn't accepted? What if the place he was trying to get to didn't exist?

A handful of brambleberries from the bushes on his path eased Simmie's hunger as he picked his way through the woods. He had always hoped to make this trip in a more casual fashion—actually buying a ticket and riding the train proper. But he was being followed, and he would hang if they caught up with him. His only hope now was to hop freight, at least for part of the trip. He could only pray that the train he caught would be going the right way.

After an hour of walking he paused, ears pricked as he heard an ominous sound off in the distance. *Dogs. Again! Dammit!* The sound was coming from the wrong direction. Did they organize a posse from another town? The freight yard must be nearby. Maybe, just maybe, he could make it and still get away. He started running. He could see rail cars through the trees. It looked like a train was just starting up. A quick sprint and he should make it to that open boxcar. The dogs were getting close. *Don't look back. Run. Just have to clear those trees.*

Out of the corner of his eye he saw a man running toward him, and before he could get out of the way, the man slammed into him, and they both tumbled to the ground. Simmie sat up and shook the dirt off his clothes. The young black man who'd run into him was lying on the ground, panting and groaning.

The barking was getting nearer, and men's voices could be heard in the distance. Simmie got to his feet, grabbed his bag, and was going to make a run for it, but the man on the ground moaned. He appeared to be around Simmie's age and was scrawny with a medium complexion, but when Simmie looked at him, all he could see was Black Pete.

"Hey!" Simmie shook him. "Get up! We gotta move!"

The man stirred and sat up.

"Let's go!" Simmie dropped his bag and pulled the man to his feet. "We got to catch that train."

They had let the dogs loose. Simmie grabbed the man by his arm, and they ran. There was no time to pick up the bag. When he glanced back, one of the hounds was already tearing at it. Another snarling animal was gaining on them. Running alongside the train, Simmie realized that it was going to take considerable effort to catch up with and jump on a train running parallel. A misstep could result in one of them getting crushed by the undercarriage. He could probably do it, but the man was barely keeping up as it was. About 100 yards ahead, the tracks took a 45-degree turn in front of them. Simmie changed direction to intercept an open boxcar.

"Where the hell you goin'?" the man panted.

"If you want to live, you better follow me!"

They sprinted, jumping switch points and junctions, until they reached the angular tracks and jumped onto a boxcar, climbing in through the open door. The big, brown bloodhound was heading straight for them, its eyes wide, tongue flying, and ears flapping in the wind. It leaped into the boxcar. The dog landed badly, sliding on its side on the smooth wooden floor until it thumped against the wall. It tried to scramble to its feet, but Simmie was quicker. The muscles in his arms bulged as he grabbed the beast by its tail and flung it along the floor and out the door. There was a yelp, then nothing. Just the sound of the wheels against the rails. *Poor dumb animal probably got caught under the wheels*, Simmie thought. He actually felt sorry about the dog but only for a moment.

Simmie sighed and squatted next to the young man, who sat wide-eyed and breathless in a corner. "So, what's your name, and why were they hot after you?"

"Y-you just threw that big dog off the train," the man said, panting.

"Guess I did. Now, are you gonna tell me who you are?"

"The name's Jefferson."

"And what'd you do?"

"Aw." Jefferson waved a hand in the air. "They sayin' I raped a white woman."

Simmie shook his head.

"I didn't rape nobody! She asked for it."

"What?" Simmie frowned.

"Missie Jane been after me for a long time. Then she called me 'round the back of the shed. We was just gettin' started when her old daddy comes up on us. Then she started yellin' rape." His eyes welled up. "Now, why she go do that?"

"If you want to keep livin,' you better stay away from white women."

"But she wanted me!"

"And you'd be one dead nigger if I hadn't been there to help you."

"You?" Jefferson said angrily. "You damn near got me caught! Runnin' into me like that!"

Simmie looked down at the bony, pathetic young man. He would have been dog food if Simmie had not saved him. He decided that it wasn't important enough to argue about. "Well, right now we need to get some rest."

He chose a spot at the other end of the car where he could see the full moon as it danced behind the passing trees. Soon both were lulled to sleep by the *clickety-clack* of the wheels on the rails and the rocking motion of the boxcar.

———————

Simmie awoke slowly and groggily. Jefferson was sitting in the corner, leaning against the wall, his arms crossed and his eyes closed. Then he realized that the train had stopped. "Get up! Gotta be ready to move."

"Why?" said an unfamiliar voice.

Simmie turned and took a step back. Sitting in the shadows in the corner was a young, sandy-haired white man in a scruffy suit coat. Simmie clenched his fist. "What are you doing here?" he growled.

"Whoa! I'm just a traveler like you, goin' to Alabama," the man said in an Irish accent.

"This train is going to Alabama?" Simmie relaxed.

"Yep, it is," the white man said. "And I hope you don't mind sharing the boxcar."

"I suppose." Simmie shrugged. "What you think?" he asked Jefferson, who was rubbing the sleep from his eyes. Just then the train started up and slowly gained speed.

"Can we trust this damned white man?" Jefferson asked.

"If I wanted to turn you boys in or somethin', I woulda done it already. You runnin' from something, right? Well, I am, too. And I won't ask if you don't ask."

"We don't need no white man travelin' with us," Jefferson sneered. "Throw him off! Like you did that other dog!"

The white man was goggle-eyed when he realized that Simmie could very easily do just that. "Now, wait a minute, fellers! You could use me! There's stuff I can do and places I can get into that you can't."

"You'd do that? You'd help us?" Jefferson asked suspiciously.

"As long as you don't throw me off."

"Ain't nobody throwing nobody off no train." Simmie sighed. "So, what's your name, mister?"

"Johnny Weeks."

"Okay, Johnny Weeks, you can stay. My name's Simmie, and this here is Jefferson. And when we get to Alabama…well, we'll see. Maybe we can help each other."

"Whatever you say, Simmie."

A few minutes later, as the train sped along, Jefferson was sound asleep again. Simmie glanced over at Johnny who sat against the wall, eyes closed. He reminded him a little of Boss Man, the white overseer at the plantation where Big Momma worked picking cotton when he was a child of about eight or nine years. He remembered watching the simple-minded overseer trying to fix a broken cotton gin. Simmie had seen the problem and the solution, but when he'd tried to help, he got slapped down by Boss Man, and Big Momma made him promise to keep his mouth shut. The next day little Simmie sneaked into the barn alone and fixed the machine. Boss Man took all the credit and told little Simmie that he would kill him and Big Momma if he ever told anyone. For years after that he'd pretended to be as dumb as the other blacks pretended to be. It wasn't until he stumbled upon the *Principia* that he finally decided he wanted to use and improve his mind. That he wanted to make something of himself and not be doomed to a life of fear and inane drudgery.

Simmie sat cross-legged and stared out the open boxcar door. He visualized calculations and drawings from his beloved *Principia*. Oblivious to the passing scenery, he drew imaginary lines and circles in the air as he quietly recited the theorems to himself.

"Let S be the focus of the ellipsis. Draw SP cutting the diameter DK of the ellipsis in E, and the ordinate Qv in x; and complete the parallelogram QxPR…"

"What are you doing?" Johnny was standing behind him.

"What? Nothing," Simmie said as he looked up at the white man.

"Nothing? Sounds like some kind of geometry to me. Now, where would a nigger like you learn somethin' like that?"

14

Simmie stood, towering a good six inches over Johnny. "What did you call me?"

Johnny backed away. "I'm sorry, friend. Didn't mean nothin' by it."

Simmie scowled as he sat back down. "You best mind your own business."

"Don't you worry. I will."

After a moment, Simmie muttered, "What do you know of geometry?"

"Only enough to recognize it when I hear it," Johnny said. "And you?"

Simmie sighed. "I was blessed with a very sharp mind. I found a copy of a book by Isaac Newton when I was a child and learned from it."

"Is that what you were reading just now?" Johnny said in amazement.

"No, that book is long gone."

"Then what…?"

"I memorized it."

Johnny walked over to where Simmie sat on the floor. "You memorized it? What are you, some kind of a genius or somethin'?"

Simmie thought for a moment. "Maybe I am. What of it?"

"Nothin'! Nothin' at all!" Johnny backed away again. "I just never heard of a nig… I mean, I never heard of a colored man being a genius, that's all. What would be the point? What the hell could you do with it, anyway?"

"I plan to continue to improve my mind. I am going to go to college."

Johnny Weeks laughed.

Simmie ignored him. "There's a college for colored men in Tuskegee, Alabama. That's where I'm headed."

"Never heard of it."

"I'm going to get a proper education."

"So, you have the money? I mean, an education is expensive."

"I'll manage." Simmie turned and stared at the passing nighttime scenery through the open door.

"Well, okay. I'll be getting some sleep now. Good night." Johnny sat back in his corner and closed his eyes.

With that, Simmie nodded off and dreamed of lines, circles, and theorems.

———————

The late afternoon sun flickered on Simmie's face as the train slowly turned this way and that through the woods. He stretched, and yawned, and looked around. Jefferson was on his back snoring, and Johnny was standing over him.

"What are you doing?" Simmie said.

Johnny's eyes were as big as saucers. "Nothin', friend. I was just checking on Jefferson here. He must have been having a bad dream…"

"What the hell? Get away from me, white man!" Jefferson stood and pushed Johnny away. As he stumbled back, a clatter of loose change bounced on the floor. Johnny quickly gathered up the few coins and thrust them into his pocket.

"Where that money come from?" Jefferson yelled, checking his pockets. "You stole from me! You took my damned money!"

"All right, Johnny Weeks," Simmie said firmly. "Give him back his money."

"I didn't take no money." Johnny took a step back.

"I said give him his money!" Simmie moved forward as Johnny edged toward the open boxcar door.

"You stay the hell away from me!" Johnny was now half out the door, hanging on with one hand. The wind whipped his hair as he looked out at the swiftly passing landscape. "I'll just be getting off here."

"Don't be a fool. We're going too fast." Simmie lunged to grab him, but Johnny vanished out of the boxcar. Simmie looked out and winced as he saw him rolling head over heels down a ravine.

"Is he dead?" Jefferson said.

"Probably." Simmie shrugged as he backed away from the door.

"Damn peckerwood. Good thang you threw his ass off. Got what he deserved."

"I didn't throw him off. I tried to save him."

"You tried to save that thievin' bastard?"

Simmie quickly rummaged through his pockets. He looked around frantically. "Uh-oh."

"What?"

"That damned white boy robbed me in my sleep. Took my money, too!"

"Goddammit!" Jefferson screamed. "You should've throwed his ass off the train the first time you saw him! Man, you ain't nothin' but bad news."

"Me?" Simmie said, dumbfounded.

"I was okay until you knocked me down back there in the woods. Then you let that goddamn white boy in, and he robs us."

Simmie sat back down and untied his right shoe, pulled off his sock, and shook out some coins. "We got enough for us to eat."

Jefferson looked at the coins in Simmie's hand. "That's all you got?"

"It's more than you got." Simmie was getting impatient. "We are just gonna have to make do, okay? So, shut up. I'm getting tired of your

16

bellyaching. We'll get off next chance we get and get us some victuals."

Jefferson went back to his corner, plopped down, crossed his arms, and scowled. A couple of hours later the train began to slow down again. Simmie peeked out the door and saw they were passing through a sizeable town. When the train stopped, they jumped off and ran across the tracks, hopped a fence, and found themselves in a small community of black people.

"Looks like we came to the right place," Simmie said, smiling. "Come on, let's get something to eat."

They came upon a little grocery store that was not much more than a shack. The owners, an elderly black couple, were very friendly to them. Simmie asked them about the Negro school in Tuskegee. They had never heard of it, but they told him the town of Tuskegee was only 50 or 60 miles away and informed him of what train he could take to get there. The two men barely had enough money for a loaf of bread. After hearing the story of their narrow escape, the wife insisted they take a small jar of strawberry jam and a frayed napkin.

They said their thank yous and goodbyes, stepped out into the scorching sun, and walked over to a big, flat rock by the side of the road, where they sat down to eat. Simmie spread the napkin out and set the bread down. Jefferson was gawking at a pretty, fair-skinned black girl, her long, brown braids waving as she sashayed barefoot down the road in a tattered calico dress. Simmie chuckled quietly as dirty, smelly Jefferson smiled at her as she passed. The girl frowned and held her nose.

"Hold this." Simmie handed Jefferson the jar, which he promptly dropped. The jar of strawberry jam now lay broken, its sweet redness oozing out over the rock.

"Goddammit, Simmie! Look what you done did now!"

"Me?" Simmie said baffled.

"All the food we had in the world," Jefferson blubbered. "All over the ground. Is you bad luck, or is you just stupid?"

Simmie had had enough. He scowled and grabbed Jefferson by the collar with one hand.

"I'm sorry!" Jefferson wailed. "Don't hurt me!"

Simmie sighed and pushed him away.

"Give me my half of the bread," Jefferson whined.

Simmie tore the loaf in half and gave one piece to Jefferson, who took the bread while wiping dirt-smudged tears from his face.

"I'm gonna go my own way," Jefferson cried as he started down the road. "And don't you be followin' me!"

"I promise," Simmie chuckled. He watched Jefferson amble down the road trying to catch up with the girl. Simmie sat down on the rock, broke off a piece of the bread, and carefully scooped up as much of the jam as he could, avoiding the bits of broken glass. He flexed his left foot in his shoe, feeling the coins and bills he had hidden in his stocking. As he sat in the warm sunshine, he tried to think of a prayer of gratitude to say before he had his breakfast, but the only words that came to mind were those of Isaac Newton:

"This most beautiful system of the sun, planets, and comets, could only proceed from the counsel and dominion of an intelligent and powerful Being. And if the fixed stars are the centers of other like systems, these, being formed by the like wise counsel, must be all subject to the dominion of One…"

Chapter 3

Chicago, Illinois

After the train rumbled away, Jimmy stood in the midsummer sun on the elevated platform and looked across the tracks down 47th Street. Stylish sculptures celebrating Bronzeville's jazz roots adorned the tops of lampposts up and down the street. Colorful plastic signs hung above old, rundown shops and storefronts. Dark-skinned boys in stark-white T-shirts stood on the corner looking downright threatening. If he'd had any sense, he'd cross over to the other platform and take the train back to 35th Street.

A young woman smiled at him as she strutted down the platform in a low-cut blouse that barely covered her full-sized bust and a short skirt that showed off her shapely legs. Jimmy stared at her cute, slightly plump face and milk-chocolate complexion and froze in a panic. Should he say something to her? What if she spoke to him? This was a geek's worst nightmare.

Loud, tinny hip-hop music cut the air. She answered her cell phone. "Who dis? Who? Where you at, bitch? Yeah, that's right! Where you been, bitch? And where my muthafuckin' money?"

He watched her walk by, screaming into the phone as she went down the stairs. After waiting for her to get to street level, he pushed through the turnstile and trotted down the steps. The heat that rose from the sidewalk was almost as bad as the sun above. Sweet smells of barbecue smoke mixed oddly with the stench of garbage ripening under the tracks. He took a deep breath, coughed, and started eastward. Though he had made a point to wear a simple T-shirt and jeans, and while he was as black as any of the other people on the street, he still felt out of place, as if somehow they could all tell he was an outsider from the suburbs. He passed a clothing store with a loud red sign above and even louder music blaring from inside. The drugstore next door looked closed until he saw customers walking out holding bags. Jimmy thought about crossing the street when he got closer to the group of young men who were talking and laughing on the corner, but decided they might think he was afraid of them, making him a more appealing target. He excused himself as he walked through the group with his head down, letting out a sigh of relief after he was several yards away and saw that no one was even looking his way.

He continued down 47th Street, sidestepping chunks of broken concrete and smashed beer bottles on the sidewalk. What the hell was Tony doing in this neighborhood?

Tony Carpenter was Jimmy's best friend. They had grown up together in the 'burbs 30-some miles south of Chicago. Many people thought Tony was some kind of whiz kid, but he wasn't that much of a genius. He himself admitted that he was just a little clever and had a strong aptitude for building things and understanding how things worked. Jimmy recalled the time when they were both 15 years old; Tony had found his dad's old broken cassette tape recorder in the basement. He studied it, took it apart, cleaned it up, and then put it back together again. It actually worked when he was done, even though there were a couple of screws and a tiny spring left over. Tony was smart enough to figure things out, careless enough to miss a few details, and lucky enough for it all to work out anyway.

After playing around with the tape recorder, Tony had become very interested in electromagnetism. "What else could be done with this magical stuff?" he'd asked Jimmy. Then one day, while browsing the "T" volume of the family's antiquated *World Book Encyclopedia*, he'd stumbled upon Nikola Tesla. Soon Tony was boring Jimmy with stories about this enigmatic wonder boy who, over a hundred years ago, was working with alternating currents, transmitting electricity through the air and even the possibility of time travel. Tony had read everything he could find on Tesla, determined to understand his work. He had even built his own Tesla coil. Jimmy was there when the thing malfunctioned and nearly burned down the Carpenter family garage, which pissed Tony's dad off something fierce.

Jimmy stopped for a minute and examined the slip of paper he had stuffed in his pocket. It was an address on South Vincennes Street. Should be just a few blocks ahead if Google was right. What was at this address, and why would Tony be waiting for him there?

Jimmy had always felt a little jealous of his friend. His dad worked for the Postal Service delivering mail, while Tony's dad was a manager at a cable TV company. Mr. Carpenter had always said that much of his success was a matter of good fortune, being in the right place at the right time, and affirmative action. That was why he was always pushing Tony to be the very best at everything. While Tony's mother was the quiet housewife who was content when the men in her life were happy, Jimmy's mom was a high school teacher who, after 15 years, seemed to be completely burned out. Tony said that he loved his parents, but he always felt a little estranged from them, because they didn't understand him. He was interested in science and technology but not nearly as bent on practical and financial success as his dad was. This bugged Jimmy; while he wanted to be as successful as Tony's father, Tony himself seemed to take his rather privileged life for granted, aspiring only to what he could easily achieve.

As he approached King Drive, Jimmy was pleasantly surprised to see the beginning of the Bronzeville Renaissance he had heard so much about. There was a beautiful, white, stone-faced building with a huge arched façade on the corner. From the train platform it looked to be some kind of church, but now he could see it was the Harold Washington Center. A majestic bronze statue of Chicago's first black mayor stood out front. A gourmet restaurant and an art gallery were located across the street. This was more like it.

Jimmy had no clue as to what he wanted to do after high school, while Tony wanted to go somewhere where he could learn more about electronics and computers, at least the stuff he didn't already know. One of the better trade schools would have worked for him. His counselors and his father would have none of that. He had the smarts to attend a world-class university and study something really useful and lucrative like engineering.

Knowing that Tesla had also been an engineer, Tony had caved in and enrolled in the electrical engineering program at Illinois Institute of Technology. Jimmy had the qualifications, so he managed to get into the same program, mostly to keep up with Tony. It turned out to be a lot more work than either had expected. Tony managed a respectable B-minus average, while Jimmy was more than happy with his C-plus. Tony would have gotten better grades had he not struggled with the theoretical concepts that he had no interest in.

One of the more useful skills he learned in high school was how to memorize and parrot back what the teachers wanted to hear. So, with a little studying and memorizing, he could pass the exams on the weirder stuff like quantum mechanics well enough and just forget it later. Besides, he figured he didn't really need to know all that advanced theoretical junk. Jimmy had to work hard for each passing grade, while Tony just seemed to skate by, enjoying success that he did not deserve.

For almost three years, Jimmy lived in the dorms with Tony just a couple of train stops north, but he had never been anywhere near this neighborhood before. The white students pretty much felt stranded, since the campus was surrounded on three sides by what was considered the "black ghetto." But the gritty urban environment was also very different from Jimmy and Tony's suburban neighborhood an hour's drive south.

As he crossed King Drive, Jimmy could see houses—a few new, some newly remodeled, many in the process of being refurbished, and the rest just seemed to be awaiting their turn for renovations. He could see now where Bronzeville was headed. Urban renewal had not yet reached the area near the train station. As Jimmy walked down a couple of blocks, things started going downhill again. He passed rundown or abandoned buildings separated by vacant lots filled with old bricks, broken bottles, and trash. His heart sank when he realized the address he was looking for was probably one of these derelicts. He once again entertained the thought of turning back, but he couldn't let his best friend down.

No one had seen Tony in several days. When his parents had called, Jimmy lied like always and told them Tony was at the library studying or in class. Tony would often disappear, sometimes for a day or two, and he would tell no one—not even Jimmy—where he had been. Rumor had it that he had a secret girlfriend who lived in the housing projects a few blocks north of the IIT campus. Somehow that did not seem likely. This time he had been incommunicado for almost a week. No one had heard from him until he called Jimmy on his cell that morning and gave him an address on Vincennes near 47th Street in what Jimmy suspected was one of the worst parts of the South Side.

Jimmy was so busy looking over his shoulder to make sure no one was following him or hiding in wait in the alleys that he nearly walked past his destination. This was the address, but it couldn't be the place. Layers of chipped red paint covered the brick and mortar, and there was a rickety-looking wooden front porch with a dozen or so steps that were white once upon a time. The two-story house had a flat front, a flat roof, and sparse ornamentation over the windows and along the cornice. It stood alone near the corner of the block. On the sides were the ghosts of rooms and stairways from the buildings with which it once had shared walls. None of this concerned Jimmy as much as the fact that most of the windows were boarded up with gray, weathered wood and that the front door and walls were covered with gang graffiti. *This can't be right,* he thought. *Must be the wrong address. This is probably the neighborhood crack house.* He turned to leave.

"Hey, Jimmy!"

Jimmy shielded his eyes from the sun as he tried to see where the voice was coming from. "Tony?"

"What took you so long?"

Jimmy spotted a pair of eyes peeking from a space between boards nailed over a window next to the front door. "You have got to be kidding! I am *not* going in there!"

"Will you just get in here?" Tony opened the door.

Jimmy sighed as he made his way up the creaking steps to the porch. He stood wide-eyed and sunblind in the darkness when Tony closed the door. "What am I doing here?" he asked no one in particular.

"You're here because you're my best friend. One of the very few people I really trust," Tony answered.

The air was comfortably cool, but it smelled of mold and mildew. Jimmy decided not to breathe too deeply.

Tony took his arm. "I have something to show you. Come on."

As Jimmy's eyes began to adjust to the semi-darkness, he noticed the layers of dust on the bits of broken furniture and trash on the floor. He shook his head as he followed Tony to a door just beyond what appeared to have once been a kitchen. When Tony opened it, Jimmy was nearly blinded again by the bright light illuminating the stairway.

"You've got power here. But how…?" Jimmy paused, deciding that he didn't want to know.

They walked down the antiquated but clean staircase to the equally well-lit basement. On one side of the room there were a couple of computers and pieces of impressive-looking electronic gear—meters, an old-fashioned oscilloscope, and other equipment—sitting on a metal table. Large sections of the wall were painted glossy white and had notes and numbers scribbled on them. On the other side were some welding tanks, a helmet, and pieces of scrap metal on the floor. What really caught his eye was the huge object covered with a tarp. It had to be close to 10 feet tall, nearly touching the ceiling. Whatever it was, it was big and appeared to be round.

"What's that?"

"In a minute," Tony said as he steered Jimmy to an old desk across the room which was covered with books, sketches, and diagrams. He handed Jimmy a small stack of papers that included a photocopy of an article called "The Theoretical Possibility of Time Travel" by Dr. Simmie L. Johnson.

Jimmy flipped through the pages.

"It's from a journal that was published over a hundred years ago. I found the book in the back of the stacks at the Hall Library, just sitting there," Tony said.

"What is this?"

Tony gave him a look of exasperation. "Will you look at it? It was written by a black scientist who came upon the greatest discovery ever! I mean, the man was a genius!"

"Time travel?" Jimmy asked flatly.

"That's what it says."

23

Jimmy stared at the papers for a moment. "So, why hasn't anyone heard about this?"

"It was published in the *Negro Journal of Science* a hundred years ago. How many people do you think read that?" Tony frowned.

"So, what are you saying?"

"I'm saying that Dr. Johnson was right. Time travel is possible. His plans for building a Chronocar are right here!" Tony excitedly turned to a page of diagrams.

Jimmy blinked. "A what?"

Tony pointed to the header on the first page of diagrams. "Chronocar. That's what Dr. Johnson called his time machine."

"So, did he build one? Has he... uh...come to see you?"

"No, he hasn't. He couldn't. There were some details he couldn't figure out. And he didn't have this." Tony ran his finger over the black box in the center of one of the drawings.

Jimmy squinted to read the small, distorted print. "Mechanical brain controller?"

"A computer! He needed a computer! And, hey, I've got computers."

"You said there was something he couldn't figure out. What was that?"

"He couldn't figure out exactly how to create and sustain a rotating electromagnetic field that could push the Chronocar through time," Tony replied. "He knew it had to be possible, and he knew it would need something like a computer to control it, but he couldn't quite work it out. I mean, the technology didn't exist, so it's no wonder he got stuck."

"And you figured it out?" Jimmy knitted his brows.

"I found some other research that I was able to apply to it...something by Nikola Tesla."

Jimmy sighed. "Tesla again?"

"Tesla once created a high-energy electrical field that allowed him to experience different timeframes."

"It was accidental, as I recall. Almost killed him, too," Jimmy said.

"I took his work and applied it to Dr. Johnson's ideas. Fit like a glove. I came up with a rotating field generator, and with the computer, I can maintain and control the field any way I want so it can move through time. I can also use a much lower power level than Tesla did, so it's a lot safer. Here, I'll show you."

He led Jimmy to the big, hump-like object and yanked off the tarp. Jimmy's jaw dropped. It was a huge, brushed-metal sphere, 10 feet or so in diameter, welded in random patchwork sections that varied slightly in color.

In the center was a small circular window two feet across and made of some sort of thick glass. The Chronocar rested on three spindly legs, just long enough to keep the bottom of the sphere from touching the floor. It vaguely reminded Jimmy of something he had seen in an old science fiction movie on TV.

"Took me six months to build this thing."

"What's this?" Jimmy gestured toward an image painted in black on the side.

"An hourglass. A stylized hourglass, I guess," Tony said, smiling. "Came up with that myself."

Jimmy frowned. "This just doesn't look like a time machine to me."

"And what is a time machine supposed to look like?"

"I don't know, like a telephone booth?"

"Very funny," Tony said.

"Wait a minute. Where did you get the money for all of this?"

"Want to look inside?" Tony said, ignoring the question.

"Tony," Jimmy said, grabbing his arm, "there must be thousands of dollars' worth of equipment and stuff down here. Where did you get the money?"

Tony took a deep breath. "Let's just say I'm going to be a little late paying tuition next semester."

"You spent your scholarship money? Man, are you crazy?" Jimmy glared at his friend in disbelief. "You're supposed to graduate next year! Your dad is going to kill you!"

"Maybe. But just imagine if this thing works…when it works!"

Jimmy let out a long sigh. "Okay. So, how *is* this damn thing supposed to work? How can it travel through time? I mean, I always thought that was impossible."

Tony explained that time was like a moving sidewalk with everyone standing on it, going along with it, passing by and through events. Traveling through time would simply require walking forward or backward on that walkway; it was just a matter of temporal velocity. Since time moved at a specific rate and direction, traveling though time would just be a matter of moving slower or faster than time itself or going in the opposite direction.

Jimmy's eyes narrowed. "So, just how fast does time move?"

Tony shrugged. "Time moves at a rate of one second per second, one minute per minute…"

"And one hour per hour?"

"Yeah, you're getting the idea. The electromagnetic field I told you about works like an engine to accelerate and direct the Chronocar through time."

"And you figured all of this out yourself?"

"No, dammit. Listen to me," Tony said. "It's all in Dr. Johnson's article. Now, I don't get all of the theory, but when I saw the plans, I knew I could build a Chronocar and make it work."

Jimmy frowned. "So, you're saying that with this thing you can just move back and forth in time all you want? Does that mean you can go and get tomorrow's lottery numbers and then come back to buy a ticket today?"

Tony laughed. "Not quite. As best I can figure, according to Dr. Johnson, you can travel back and forth in the past all you want, but you can't go to the future, because it does not exist yet. Remember that moving walkway? It's constantly being constructed right in front of us with a sort of wall that keeps us from going forward and…I don't know…falling off or something. We can move back and forth all we want on the sidewalk behind us, because that part has already been created. But if we try to go forward beyond the present, well…we would hit that wall."

"Wait a second," Jimmy pondered. "I saw this program on the Discovery Channel. Stephen Hawking said just the opposite—that if time travel were possible, you would only be able to go to the future. And it would be a one-way trip."

"Hey, I don't know. Who says he can't be wrong? All I know is that this thing is going to work, and if Dr. Johnson and Tesla are right, I can travel through time."

"So, we couldn't get tomorrow's lottery numbers, but we could go back to last Saturday, get those numbers, then go back to last Friday and buy the ticket."

"Yeah, I guess we could!" Tony grinned.

"I'm sorry. This just doesn't make any kind of sense."

"Look, I'll try to explain at least the part of the theory I think I understand."

Jimmy sat on the edge of the desk, moving papers aside to make room. "Okay, I'm listening."

Tony walked over to one of the glossy white sections of the wall and wiped some notes and calculations off with an eraser. He drew images and diagrams as he spoke. Just as Einstein had said, time and space were interrelated. When you traveled through space, you naturally traveled through time. When you traveled great distances at high speed, time—relative to you—worked differently. When you traveled through time, space behaved differently relative to you. That was where transposition came in. When you moved forward or backward through time, you were automatically transposed to a different point in space while traveling.

"That's why the Chronocar is airtight and has oxygen and air scrubbers," Tony said. "While moving through time, the Chronocar will also be traveling through space."

"Wait," Jimmy chuckled dryly. "Outer space?"

"Right," Tony said matter-of-factly. "During a time journey, the traveler is supposed to get transposed to another point in space. The distance of the transposition depends on how far and how fast he's traveling. When the trip is over, he's transposed back."

Jimmy felt like his head was going to explode. "Explain this transposition thing. I don't get it."

"When you travel through space at high speed," Tony continued, "weird things happen to time relative to you. When you travel through time at high speed, strange things happen to space relative to you. I know it's crazy and hard to follow. Can't say I totally understand it. I just know that when you travel through time, you get instantly transposed or moved to another point in space. The computer will help compute where in space you should be when the time trip is over. So you end up in the same spot on the planet."

Jimmy stared blindly at him.

"Okay, let me break it down so even you will understand." Tony said. He told him to think of a phonograph record and to imagine the last song was playing. If you wanted to start the record again from the beginning, you would lift the needle and place it in the first groove. "Get it now?"

"Nah, nah," Jimmy protested with a grin. "It won't work. You overlooked something."

"No, I haven't. What have I overlooked?"

"You!"

"What are you talking about?"

"You! If you move back in time, you'll get younger and younger. As a matter of fact, once you go back far enough, parts of the machine will start to disappear until…"

"No." Tony shook his head. "I've got that covered with the Tesla field."

"The what?" Jimmy said flatly.

"That's the electromagnetic field I was talking about. The Chronocar will be surrounded by it. It propels the Chronocar in time, and it also contains the time inside. I won't get older or younger; I won't be affected by the changing time outside at all. Neither will the Chronocar. No matter what time I go to, it will still be now—July 26, 2015—inside the Tesla field."

Jimmy glowered at his friend. "Got it all figured out, don't you?"

Tony gestured toward the metal sphere. They walked around to the rear of the Chronocar where a large oval cutout served as the door that had another round window near the top. There was an audible hissing sound when Tony turned the door handle. "Take a look inside."

Jimmy hesitated.

"You must really think I'm crazy," Tony said. "Hey, I understand. I mean, people thought the Wright Brothers were crazy, and Tesla, well, I guess he was a little nuts. You might say that I'm in pretty good company!" Tony laughed. "Go on. Get in. Just don't touch anything."

Jimmy climbed in. Attached to the floor was an upholstered seat that looked as if it had come from the front of an SUV. A harness was bolted to the curved ceiling to be used as a seat belt. He maneuvered around and sat in the chair. Before him was a computer keyboard, a trackball mouse, and a 20-inch flat screen monitor. A small panel in the desktop next to the keyboard contained an unfathomable array of switches, knobs, and LEDs labeled with letters and numbers. The room outside was visible through the little round window, slightly dimmed and magnified by the thickness of the glass.

Tony reached around Jimmy, flipped a couple of switches, and the Chronocar came to life. The interior lit up, and the little LED bulbs twinkled on the console. After a few seconds, the computer booted up. Tony tapped the keyboard a few times and moved away. Jimmy was trying to make sense of the computer screen display when he heard the door close and the lock engage. At the same moment, the computer began to emit rhythmic beeps. He scanned the displays on the monitor until he found one that sent a chill down his spine. It was counting down seconds with less than 20 to go. Another window displayed the time and date: "July 26, 2015, 16:00 CDT," which was 4:00 p.m. in military time. According to his phone, it was a little after 2:00 p.m. The computer clock was wrong. Unless… He looked at the screen more closely. It was not a clock display; it was a destination! The time machine was set to travel two hours into the future.

He looked up and saw Tony through the glass. He was watching him, waiting for something. "Hey! Hey!" Jimmy yelled. Either Tony was ignoring him or he could not hear him. At 10 seconds in the countdown, there was a high-pitched electronic whine, its frequency increasing with each moment until it faded beyond his perception.

The beeping stopped. One of the windows on the computer read:
Tesla Field Engaged
There were some incomprehensible numbers, as well. He suddenly got

28

the distinct feeling that the Chronocar was floating. Was this for real? What if it was and something went wrong? Where—or when—would he end up? He jumped when he heard what sounded like an electric motor and gears engaging below. Then he detected the faint smell of something overheating, burning. He climbed out of the harness, undid the latch on the door, and pushed. The door opened a few inches. He banged it. It was blocked. He couldn't get out. He could not see anything through the window that could be keeping the door from opening. It had to be something that was just out of sight.

He flinched when the computer made a loud buzz, and he turned to look at the screen:

Temporal Transposition Error.
Fail-Safe Engaged.
System Shutdown.

The mechanical sounds faded, and the computer screen went blank. Using all his strength, Jimmy rammed the door with his shoulder. It flew open, and he spilled out onto the floor, banging his head against a wall. He could hear Tony laughing on the other side of the Chronocar.

"Dammit, man! What's with you?" Jimmy groaned as he got up. "You're crazy, Tony! You're crazy!" He walked around the machine, rubbing the sore spot on his head.

"Did you see what happened?" Tony giggled.

"What I saw was this contraption rattle, make a lot of noise, and almost catch on fire!" Jimmy yelled. "And I saw my best friend try to kill me by blocking the door so I couldn't get out!"

"I didn't block the door." Tony glowered for a second. "That was the Tesla field. It surrounds the Chronocar a few inches from the surface. It's invisible."

"Don't lie to me! Whatever it was, it was hard and solid." Jimmy's eyes narrowed as he clenched his hands into fists.

Tony held up his hands in surrender and took a step back. "The Tesla field is a time barrier. Nothing can penetrate it. Absolutely nothing. That's what was blocking the door. When it shut down, you were able to get out, right?"

Jimmy relaxed and gazed at Tony, wondering what his poor mother would say when she found out that the pride of the Carpenter family had gone stark-raving nuts.

"Sorry. I needed to do a final test from outside the machine. I needed to see how well the Tesla field performed while someone was inside. And it worked perfectly. It did exactly what it was supposed to do," Tony said, grinning. "Well, it's time to go."

"Go? Go where?"

"I'm going to go see Dr. Johnson and show him my—or rather, his—creation. I'm going to today's date in the year 1919. That's the only time I know for sure that he lived in Chicago, right here in this house."

"Now, wait a minute," Jimmy protested. "You just saw that thing rattle and smoke. It don't work, man."

"You haven't been paying attention," Tony said as he started gathering cans of soda and bags of snacks. "What was it set for? The future, right? What did I just tell you about traveling to the future?"

"You can't go to the future, because it doesn't exist yet?" Jimmy recited softly.

"I wanted to check it out with you inside, but I didn't want to send you back in time. When the Chronocar tried to go to the future, it hit the wall I told you about. It would have burned itself out if it weren't for the fail-safe that automatically shut it down. So, it worked perfectly. That was the final test. Now for the real thing." Tony climbed in, putting the cans of soda and snacks into a plastic cooler. "The trip is going to take about two hours," he called from inside.

"It's going to take two hours to travel to 1919?" Jimmy said, his head spinning.

"Don't want to push it too hard on the first trip." Tony stepped out of the Chronocar and approached Jimmy. "Well, this is it. I'm leaving. I might stay for a few days, but I should be back around six o'clock tonight. Why don't you come back here then?"

"Six o'clock tonight?" Jimmy said blankly.

"Look, you are going to be my witness. You're going to see me and the Chronocar disappear. Then you'll see me reappear in four hours, with stories to tell, and…" he held up his smartphone, "with lots of pictures to show. I'll need you to help back up my story."

Jimmy shook his head. "You can't do this. I mean, if this thing works—if it *really* works, you could change history. You know, *Back to the Future*? You could do something that…prevents you from being born or something."

"Finally, you're believing me. But that's not how it works. I mean, this isn't some crazy sci-fi movie. This is reality."

"I just don't understand," Jimmy muttered.

Tony tried another analogy. Time, he said, was like a long piece of recording tape that was being recorded as we experienced the present. If you were to go back in time—rewind the tape—you could "replay" the past. But the recording was fixed. You couldn't change what had already happened. And even if you changed the beginning of a tape recording, it would not affect what was recorded later.

Jimmy stared at him wide-eyed. Weirdly enough, it was all starting to make sense. "I think I understand. You're scaring the crap out of me, Tony."

"I have to get going. I need you to help back up my story when I return, but you can't stay here."

"Why not?"

"When I leave, I'm going to transpose somewhere in space," Tony explained. "Well, it works both ways. Whatever is there will transpose here. That would be a vacuum the size of the Chronocar. You don't want to be here when that happens."

Jimmy watched as Tony climbed inside for the last time. He honestly didn't know what to think.

"Go on! Get outta here. Come back in 10 minutes, and you'll see that I've gone." Tony closed the door and sealed himself in.

Jimmy ran up the steps, through the dusty old rooms, and out into the blinding sunlight. He walked around to the side of the building and found a small window to the basement where he could see the Chronocar inside. *What if it just sits there and does nothing like before? What if it catches fire and burns the building down? What if it explodes?* With that thought, he backed away from the building and went across the street, where he could still see part of the Chronocar through the basement window.

The hot July sun caused little rivers of perspiration to roll down his face. Jimmy wiped his brow, squinting to keep the silver sphere in view. A drop of sweat trickled into his eye. He blinked it away. Just then the old building collapsed in a thick gray cloud of choking dust that engulfed the street as people screamed and ran. When it settled, all that was left of the old house was a pile of rubble.

No one believed Jimmy's story about his friend and the time machine. And it was no wonder. The firemen picked through the debris and found no body and no evidence of the Chronocar. All they found were the remains of some expensive test equipment and some old human bones that were buried under the floor in the cellar. The TV news made a bigger story of the century-old skeleton, possibly some tantalizing murder mystery from the past.

As for the building itself, everyone said that it was a natural gas explosion. Some guy even claimed to have smelled gas coming from the building a few minutes before. But Jimmy knew the truth. He had played back those last few moments in his mind over and over again. The building did not explode. The wooden boards over the windows did not blow out—they blew in. The walls caved inward, and the building fell straight down. That was an implosion. An implosion caused by the sudden, violent rush of air closing an immense vacuum.

And the most compelling vision of all was that of the Chronocar. For the briefest instant, just as he opened his eyes after blinking away the drop of sweat—for perhaps the shortest period of time that the human brain could perceive, a fraction of a second—Jimmy had seen, without a doubt, that Tony and the Chronocar had vanished.

Chapter 4

Tony climbed into the Chronocar and belted himself in. Through the thick-paned glass, he saw Jimmy head for the stairs. The computer was patiently waiting for the next command. His hands trembled as he entered the parameters into the program and determined that all was working properly. According to the computer displays, dials, switches, and indicator lights everything was in perfect working order. The bravado that he'd put on for Jimmy a few minutes before was gone; this was the moment of truth, and it scared the hell out of him. All it would take now was a simple keystroke, and he would be on his way. Or not. Jimmy should be safe outside by now, watching, waiting for something to happen. He couldn't back out now. He'd put in too much time and invested too much money. *This is going to work. It has to work.* Tony took a deep, shaky breath and smartly tapped the enter key.

For what seemed like an eternity, nothing happened. Then a faint hum from below—the gyrostabilizer was spinning up. The computer did its 20-second countdown as Tony heard the whine of the condensers for the Tesla field generator charging. After that came the strange floating sensation when the Tesla field engaged. It was out of his hands now. From this point, it was all automatic, controlled by the second-hand PC he had rebuilt and modified.

Tony watched as his lab melted away, replaced by his own multiple reflections that peered back at him dimly from the thick, layered glass. The harness kept him in his seat, but he could feel the sensation of weightlessness in his stomach and head. As he raced back through time, he had been instantaneously transposed to some point in space. He switched off the lights and was startled by the stark beauty of infinity. The stars were countless, separated by absolute blackness. Where was Earth? The moon? Must be above or below him, just out of sight, he reasoned.

Space travel had been a childhood dream, and he had been looking forward to it once he decided to build the Chronocar. Now he was in space, probably somewhere just beyond the moon, but no one knew where he was. If anything went wrong now, even if they knew where to find him, what could they do? Send a Soyuz? Even that wouldn't help, because he wasn't just traveling through space—he was traveling through time. If he got stuck out here, the only thing that could save him would be another time machine, and so far as he knew, he had the only one.

He had checked and double-checked everything. Yes, many of the systems had redundancies, and everything appeared to be running smoothly, so there was no reason to worry. Everything was going to be fine.

He hoped.

Wait, he thought. Something was not right. The stars seemed to be moving right to left ever so slowly. That shouldn't be happening unless, of course, the Chronocar was rotating. About a quarter of a revolution per minute, he guessed. The gyrostabilizer, which was supposed to prevent the spinning, was apparently running a little under speed. Well, no big deal. The spin was so slight that he figured it wouldn't pose a real problem. The computer was easily keeping up with the changes. Besides, maybe the earth and moon would eventually come into view. That was something he was dying to see.

He stared out of the window at the stars. What if something did go wrong? What if his calculations were off? What if he ended up someplace other than Dr. Johnson's house in 1919? Lost forever in time and space. What if he could not figure out how to get back home? What if…? *Okay, get a grip,* he thought, and turned the light back on.

Damn!

The wire on the mouse was stretched tight as it hovered in the air. Anything that was not fastened down was adrift. He thought he had been careful to secure everything—the computer to the desk and the monitor to the computer—but clearly, he had missed a few items. The big plastic cooler that contained the snacks was almost a foot above the floor and open, its contents floating out.

He opened the drawer under the console. A roll of duct tape hovered up toward him. He spent the next several minutes taping things down: the mouse, the keyboard, the cooler and its cover. After that, he picked junk out of the air—errant screws, paper clips, a small Allen wrench he had lost a week earlier—and secured them in the drawer.

But now, the zero gravity was making him feel queasy. He opened the cooler and grabbed a can of soda. Ginger ale. Yeah, that should help settle his stomach. He pulled the ring on the pop-top, and the contents of the can exploded in his face, spraying all over the place. No, not all over the place—all *in* the place! In seconds the air inside the Chronocar was full of tiny globules of clear, sticky-sweet liquid.

He tried to cover the opening of the can with his finger. The stuff was everywhere. Little undulating bubbles of soda floated around like transparent insects. Some were as big as marbles. Others were as tiny as dust, stinging his eyes. He could feel them on his arms and in his hair as they splattered against the walls, table, keyboard, monitor, and computer.

He released the empty can and waved his hands frantically, trying to direct the liquid away from the equipment. The cooling fan in front of the computer was sucking in the droplets. He placed a few paper napkins secured by tiny bits of silver tape over the computer and the other equipment. He undid the harness and waved napkins broadly in the air, trying to capture as many of the soda bubbles as possible. Then he wiped the stuff up as best he could, hanging onto the seat to keep from floating around.

Both windows were a little smeared from the soda, but he could still see out pretty clearly. Half an hour later it was about as clean as it was going to get, but everything was still a sticky mess, including him. He removed the paper shield that covered the computer, placed the damp, tacky napkins inside the drawer, and taped it shut.

"God, that was stupid!" He sighed as he strapped himself back into the harness, his clothes sticking uncomfortably to his skin. With an hour of transposition to go, he decided the best thing to do would be to just relax and watch the stars. Stay out of trouble.

He turned off the light. The stars were moving by faster. Instead of once every few minutes, the Chronocar was rotating at what seemed like two or three revolutions per minute. But this was not what alarmed him. There was no sign of the earth or the moon. He glanced out of the window in the door behind him. No Earth or moon there either. Where was he? He must be a hell of a lot farther away from home than he thought. Now he was really scared.

One of the passing stars looked awfully bright. With each rotation it seemed to get larger and brighter. Impossible! He would have to be traveling many times the speed of light to be approaching any star that quickly. It wasn't long before it was clear that this was not a star but a planet. Its reversed orbital speed was exaggerated by the fact that the Chronocar was traveling backward through time at a rate of almost 50 years per hour. He could almost make out details on its surface. It had only a wisp of an atmosphere and was a deep, mesmerizing blue. Could it be Neptune? Could he be that far out? Whatever it was, it was getting uncomfortably close.

The numbers on the computer monitor changed rapidly, trying to keep up as the Chronocar spun out of control. Occasionally the whirling numbers would hesitate for a moment. Tony feared this was an indication that it was working with incomplete data and not keeping up with the changes in velocity caused by the spinning. He needed to do something.

It had to be the gyrostabilizer, an old army surplus device he had modified. He had tested it several times, and it checked out fine. It was designed for an aircraft many times the size of the Chronocar, so it simply had to work. But it wasn't working. It wasn't preventing the Chronocar from spinning wildly in space. Worse, it was one of the few systems that did not have a backup. Tony cringed at the thought of what he would have to do. The unit was located behind a plate on the bottom of the sphere, requiring him to go outside to fix it. The Tesla field that surrounded the ship should protect him like a big, invisible glass bubble, keeping the air in so he wouldn't need a space suit, which was good, because he didn't have one.

He called up the Tesla field control program on the computer, knowing that by doing this the other functions would all but cease; the little computer was already working its chips off. The field itself was maintained by other circuitry, but the computer had to be used to give the complex commands to control and modify it. According to the computer, the Tesla field was being maintained at a distance of about six inches from the Chronocar's skin. At that setting, he wouldn't be able to open the door. He expanded the field diameter to four feet from the surface of the sphere, knowing that when the field was stretched, it became weaker and the chance of a breakdown increased exponentially.

Tony stared out of the window into empty space, took a deep breath, then another. Then he undid the latch on the door. He pushed it open slowly, prepared to pull it shut if there was any sign of air escaping. The door opened a little and stopped. He tried to force it. No luck. The Tesla field must have still been set at six inches. What the hell?

He looked at the computer screen, and his heart sank. The numbers and indicators that should have been changing were not. When he moved the mouse, the cursor was defiantly unresponsive. The damned thing had locked up. He was going to have to reboot the computer.

The systems could run without the computer. It just sent the commands to make changes and adjustments. But he had never tested any of it with the computer offline. Now he had no choice but to hit Control-Alt-Delete. Nothing. Again, again, and again—still nothing. He swallowed hard, then pressed and held the power button. The screen went black. He imagined everything from a voltage spike to hard drive failure. Did it overheat while he had the vents covered with the paper napkins? Could some of the soda have gotten into the vents and shorted something? What if some of the sticky liquid had gotten into the hard drive? What if he got the dreaded "blue screen of death" and the computer simply stopped working altogether? There were millions of microscopic wires inside the processor. If a surge melted just one of them, he'd be stranded in space forever.

He turned the computer back on. It beeped, and white text scrolled up the screen. When the Windows logo finally appeared, he thanked God and Bill

Gates, in that order. This time, the computer accepted and executed the commands perfectly.

The Tesla field was absolutely impenetrable. It was also quite invisible, and Tony nearly vomited when he opened the door and looked outside into empty space. He slammed the door shut and held on to the chair so he would not float around inside. After all, he reasoned, if the Tesla field was not working, he would have been sucked out into space as soon as he opened the door and would have been dead seconds later. It took every nerve he had to open the door again and push himself out of the Chronocar, bumping into the field, and getting a painful jolt on his hand. He crawled along the metal skin, grabbing bolts and weld joints to avoid the field, but his stomach churned at the sight of floating and spinning in space with no visible means of support.

The planet was gigantic, and it was getting closer as it swung in and out of view. He swallowed hard again and made his way to the bottom of the Chronocar. Wrapping his arm around one of the legs for support, he removed a few small screws with the trusty little Allen wrench and pulled off the plate. The gyrostabilizer unit appeared to be humming away perfectly, running at what seemed to be the right speed. And yet the Chronocar was still spinning. He didn't dare touch the unit for fear that any disturbance might cause it to spin even more or completely lose control. After replacing the plate, he clambered his way back up, and when the door rotated within reach, he climbed back in and snapped it shut. He deliberately took several deep, slow breaths and changed the Tesla field back to its proper setting.

Termination of transposition was set to happen in about 10 minutes when the time trip would end and he would appear at his destination. Tony feared he would reach the big, blue planet long before then. Was he even inside the solar system? A hundred million miles or a hundred billion miles from home, it didn't seem to make much difference.

Five minutes to go. It seemed like all that would be left of Tony and his time machine would be a shallow crater on some godforsaken planet. A few keystrokes on the computer could abort the transposition and end the trip, but then he wouldn't be sure of where, or when, he would end up.

The planet was now so close that it filled the window when it passed. He entered the commands to place the system into abort mode, and a single keystroke would now kick him out of transposition and force him to land somewhere. But he could end up in an unidentifiable time and place with no point of reference to help him find his way home. He thought about his parents. To them, he would have vanished without a trace. Just another missing person. And what about poor Jimmy? No one would ever believe him.

Two minutes of transposition left. Good thing this was a slow-moving planet, but there was now the problem of relative position. Even if he could hold out and exit transposition normally, his position in space might have changed as a result of this encounter. It was very likely that the Chronocar was already in the gravitational field of this monster. That, along with the spinning, would mean that his final position after transposition might not be correct. The little PC would have to do some quick work to keep up with the constant changes, and he couldn't be sure if it was doing the job.

Thirty seconds left. Tony's finger hovered over the abort command key. What could be worse: to be lost forever in time and space or to die quickly on some desolate planet? He strapped himself in.

Twenty seconds. The Chronocar was spinning faster. The view of the planet made him dizzy as it blurred past.

Ten seconds. A hopeful thought crossed his mind. If the Tesla field remained intact, the Chronocar would not actually crash. It would either bounce off or sink, depending on the composition of the planet's surface. If he was going fast enough, he might even punch through it. If that happened, maybe he could still manage to get to 1919 or back home.

The Chronocar shuddered violently. Tony's harness snapped, and he was thrown from his seat, tumbling uncontrollably inside the vehicle, thrashing about like clothes in a dryer. Gravity suddenly took hold. Something went *crack* on the back of his head, and he blacked out.

Chapter 5

Tony sat up in the near darkness. He rubbed a sore spot on the back of his skull and felt a warm stickiness. What did he hit his head on? He must have crash-landed on that big, blue planet a gazillion miles from home. The Chronocar had landed nearly upright, but it appeared to be pretty badly damaged. The computer seemed to be in one piece, but switches and lights on the control panel were broken off, and there was obviously no power. If he were on Neptune or somewhere crazy like that, there wouldn't be a breathable atmosphere. He had enough food to last him a day or two, but with no power, the air scrubbers would not be working, and he only had enough oxygen to last an hour or so. Here he was, the first man ever to make his way into deep space, and no one would ever know. At least, not for a very long time. Hundreds of years in the future perhaps someone would find his bones and wonder how he'd gotten here.

He wouldn't have time to fix all the damage before he ran out of breathable air. Still, he had to try. There did not seem to be any air leaks, so maybe there was some hope. He inhaled deeply to try to calm his nerves but caught himself; he needed to conserve fresh air. He unstrapped the harness and slowly stood, his bones creaking. As he did, he felt the Chronocar shift; he guessed it was probably precariously balanced at the edge of some bottomless abyss. With the power gone, there would be no Tesla field to protect him. Moving cautiously, he shifted his weight as he felt the ship move.

He pulled himself up to the window. It appeared that the Chronocar was inside a solid object. No, not completely solid. There was a two-inch ribbon of light at the top of the window. On closer inspection, he could see that the solid object that covered most of the glass was a floor. He could see the bottom of a bed, a chair, and some other furniture. He was looking into a room above from the perspective of a cockroach. The Chronocar had transposed several feet below floor level. So, he was somewhere on Earth—or perhaps some other inhabited planet.

Just then the time machine groaned and slipped. He braced himself as the sliver of light vanished and the floor moved up and away. The Chronocar fell about 10 feet and for a second he was weightless once more until it landed with a tremendous crash. He rubbed his back and picked himself up from the floor. At least the vehicle seemed to be stable now. He made his way back to the window. The dust was still settling, but he knew exactly where he was. He was in the parlor of the very same house on Vincennes Street.

He climbed out of the Chronocar and tried to clear his head. The dust-covered furniture and fixtures looked old-fashioned but new. Above him the Chronocar had left a large, perfectly round hole in the ceiling.

"Daddy! Daddy! What happened? Is the house falling in?" a female voice shrieked from around a corner. Just then a lovely dark-skinned young woman ran into the room and froze when she saw Tony and the Chronocar, which filled nearly half the room. She was thin, dressed in what must have been the height of early 20th-century fashion—a white, billowy blouse with long puffed sleeves and a long, dark skirt, so long that he could barely make out the black lace-up shoes below. Her cottony black hair was gathered on the top of her head. She glared at Tony, then at the Chronocar, and ran back out screaming louder than before. Tony stepped back, leaned against the machine, and tried to gather his wits.

A tall, somewhat frail-looking middle-aged man with a medium-dark complexion, short white hair, and a pair of wire-rimmed glasses entered the room. He turned and saw the time machine, and his knees buckled. Tony rushed to his side and took his arm. "Are you okay, sir?"

"I'll be fine," the man said as he tried to regain his composure. "Just a little bit of a shock. Do you have a message for me?"

"A message? I don't know what you mean."

"You get away from my father!" The young woman was back. This time she was armed with a cast iron skillet.

"No, Ollie! Don't!" the elderly man said in a weak voice.

"Whoa!" Tony backed away. "I was just trying to help!"

"I said get away!" Ollie swung the pan at Tony, barely missing his head.

"Hey, I'm not…"

She swung again, striking his shoulder.

"Ow!" Tony cried. She charged again. This time he caught the weapon, snatched it out of her hand, and tossed it to the floor. He grabbed her around the waist from behind. "Calm down! I'm not going to hurt anybody!"

Ollie wriggled out of his grasp. The last thing Tony remembered was her fist in his face.

———◆◆◆———

Tony opened his eyes. As his vision cleared he recognized the pretty young woman who had punched his lights out. She was now wearing a yellow sundress, and her hair was wrapped in a scarf. He was lying on some sort of ornate couch in a turn of the century room. The Chronocar was visible through the doorway in the next room.

"No, don't move!" Ollie pleaded. "I'm so sorry I hit you. I was just trying to protect my father."

40

"She meant no harm," the old man said. "When you tried to help me, she thought…"

"That's okay." Tony sat up. "You pack a hell of a punch! Ollie, right?" He rubbed his jaw.

"Ollie, that's right." She gave him a faint smile.

"And you are Dr. Johnson?" Tony asked the thin, white-haired man.

"Yes, Dr. Simmie Johnson. And who are you?"

"Tony Carpenter is my name. Tell me, what is today's date?"

"It is July 26, 1919," Dr. Johnson said. "Six o'clock in the afternoon. Was this your intended destination?"

"Wow! I mean, yes, this is exactly right. I can't believe it, after all the problems I had…"

"Daddy said you were from the future."

"Yeah. This date in the year 2015," Tony replied.

"You don't look like you come from 2015." Ollie frowned.

"How should I look?" Tony grinned.

"Futuristic, I guess," she said. "I mean, you look like an ordinary man. Even your clothes. Except for the strange picture on your shirt."

"Are you feeling well enough to show us around your ship?" Dr. Johnson asked eagerly.

"It's your invention, Dr. Johnson. I built it according to your plans."

"It is a Chronocar, yes." The doctor smiled. "It is an incredible machine! I looked around a little, and I have many questions."

Tony winced as he stood up. "I have questions for you, too."

The three of them gingerly stepped over debris as they made their way through the parlor. The portal on the Chronocar was open, and Tony was surprised to see the computer screen and a few of the panel lights lit up.

"I took the liberty of poking around," Dr. Johnson said as he followed Tony inside. "I found a loose wire inside the cabinet here." He laid a hand on the top of the panel. "When I reconnected it, everything lit up. Including your, um, controller here."

Tony scanned the monitor screen. As best as he could tell, the computer appeared to be working. He would still have to go through everything to get the Chronocar operational again.

"Just how does your controller work?" the doctor asked. "It looks rather sophisticated."

"You mean the computer? That's a long story."

"It's wonderful," Ollie chimed in.

"Ollie, please go set up the cot in the basement for Tony. He will need a place to sleep."

"Yes, Daddy," she said in a disappointing tone.

"I promise I will show you around the Chronocar later." Tony grinned at her.

Her face lit up with a smile as she walked away.

Tony proceeded to explain how he solved some of the technical issues in building the Chronocar, including the ideas he got from Tesla that made the Tesla field possible. Dr. Johnson seemed impressed with this, telling Tony how he had read that the great Nikola Tesla had recently fallen on hard times. The doctor seemed to follow everything that Tony described, even some of the complex technology of the computer, which did not surprise him, really. The man, after all, was a genius by any standards.

"I do have a question for you," Tony said. "Under the floor here is a gyrostabilizer. A gyroscope device that is supposed to help keep the Chronocar from rolling and spinning."

"Yes, invented a few years ago by a Mr. Sperry. I am familiar with it."

"Oh. Well, mine looked like it was working perfectly, but the Chronocar still spun out of control. That's why I landed halfway between your first and second floor. I don't understand what the problem was."

The doctor thought for a moment. "Reverse," he said. "You were traveling backward through time. It would have to run in reverse to work."

"Of course!" Tony thumped his forehead. "Then I'll be able to get it all straightened out so I can go back home later after we have had a little visit. Just have to do a little rewiring."

Dr. Johnson sat in the seat and looked up at Tony. "Tell me, with all of time available to you, why did you choose to come here? Why now?"

Tony explained that it seemed logical to show the Chronocar to its inventor on the first time-trip. He had had a very difficult time locating Dr. Johnson. His research revealed a surprising number of men named Simmie Johnson. He was only able to narrow it down in 1918, when Dr. Johnson bought the house on Vincennes Street. The age seemed right, and he was the only Simmie Johnson who had "doctor" written in front of his name. Tony figured it would be best to visit in 1919, a year after Dr. Johnson had bought the house, thinking that he would be settled in by then. He had decided to visit during the summer when the weather was good. He had checked newspapers online and in the library and found that the summer of 1919 was a relatively uneventful time. There would be some racial problems sometime in late August with people fighting in the streets, but the biggest news story was a scandal involving the Chicago White Sox baseball team, and even that would not happen until the fall.

"Yes, I see," the doctor said. "You seem to have done your homework."

"Well, I tried. No way I can know everything about this time, so I'm still looking forward to learning a lot, especially about you."

Dr. Johnson turned to him. "What do you know of me?"

"That's just it… almost nothing," Tony said. "I read your article in that journal, and it blew me away!"

"Blew you away?"

"Let's say that I was extremely impressed," Tony chuckled. "I read somewhere that you got your degree at Tuskegee. And that's about all I could find."

"Good," the doctor whispered.

"What?" Tony said. "Don't you want to be known for your work?"

"You talk of notoriety. I'm only the son of a slave. I'm actually damned lucky to just be alive."

Tony listened enraptured as the doctor told him the story of his escape from certain death by lynching almost 30 years earlier, and how his chance discovery of Isaac Newton's book changed his life and ultimately led to his dream to attend the Tuskegee Institute.

"That's where you got your PhD?"

"Well, yes…" The doctor suddenly changed the subject and inquired about how sticky everything was inside the Chronocar. Tony explained what had happened with the soda in zero gravity as he rubbed the sore spot on the back of his neck. "And I am afraid that part of your ceiling is probably lying on a planet a few million miles from here," he added.

"I did wonder about that," Dr. Johnson said with a grin. "Luckily that is a spare room, and no one was in there."

"I'll help you clean up your… What did you call it?" Ollie was back, peeking through the door.

"Chronocar." Tony smiled as he looked into her dark brown eyes. She was actually quite lovely.

"Look, Tony, I think you need to rest," Ollie said. "You boys can play more later."

"She's right. You get some sleep. I'd say you could use a bath, too. You can tell me more about your trip afterwards."

"I could use some rest," Tony agreed, then he turned to the doctor. "You know, you don't seem to be too surprised to see me or the Chronocar. Neither of you."

The doctor gave him a strange look. "Well," he grinned, "I figured sooner or later someone would figure out how to build one, and I was kind of hoping they—you—would come to visit me. And I told Ollie all about the possibility that we might get a visitor from the future a couple of years ago."

"I never dreamed that our time-traveling visitor would be a colored man," Ollie interrupted. "What happened to your head?"

"You punched me, remember?"

"No, I mean in the back there."

"Oh, I hit it on something when I crashed. It's nothing."

"Nothing? There's blood all over the back of your neck! You come with me."

At her beckoning, Tony climbed out of the dust-covered Chronocar.

"Don't worry, I won't touch anything," Dr. Johnson said as Ollie took Tony by the arm.

She pulled him into the bathroom, a surprisingly large space with a sink, pull-chain toilet, claw-foot tub, and white ceramic-tiled floor. She opened a cabinet above the sink and grabbed a little bottle of dark red liquid that she poured onto a piece of cotton.

"Turn around and let me see," she said. Tony jumped and yelped as she cleaned the wound. "Be still, now."

"Ow! That hurts!"

"I said be still! I heard you tell my father that you had done research about us. You must know everything about us and this time."

"Not really," he winced. "I mean, I studied your father's plans and theories enough to build the Chronocar. It was tricky actually finding him. I didn't even know he had a daughter. Where is your mother?"

"She died when I was a small child," Ollie said softly.

"Sorry. Well, anyway, I did enough research, skimmed enough newspapers and magazines to know that this would be a safe time to visit. I mean, you're not in the middle of a war or anything."

"The war ended last year."

"Yeah, right. So, I guess I know enough to sort of get by, but I figured I would learn more while I was here."

Ollie finished cleaning his wound. "I guess you'll be all right now." She put the cotton and bottle of medicine into the cabinet and turned to face him. "So, tell me about your future. What's it like?"

Tony reached into his pants pocket and pulled out his cell phone.

Ollie furrowed her brows in confusion. "What's that?"

"A phone. You have telephones, right?"

"We don't have one, but I have seen them. That tiny thing can't be a

44

telephone. Where's the wire?"

"It's a phone with no wires. And it's a camera, too. I'll show you." He stepped back a couple of feet and pointed it at her. She jumped at the flash.

"It's okay. I just took your picture. Look." He turned the screen toward her.

"Oh, my God! And it's all color! It's a miracle!"

"No," Tony said. "Future technology."

"Can I see?" She sat down on the edge of the bathtub and examined the device. "Show me how the telephone part works."

"It won't work here, but I can show you more pictures." Tony sat next to her and cycled through the pictures of his family and friends as he told her about life in the future. Televisions that allowed you to see moving pictures in color without having to go to a theater. When she did not seem to get that, he showed her a video of Jimmy playing table tennis with some guy and explained that back home he could view movies on a screen five feet wide. He tried to explain computers and the Internet, but it was a bit too much for her to grasp.

"So, if you are all so advanced, then I bet you don't have any sickness anymore, right? I bet you don't have any wars or poverty, either!" There was excitement in her voice. "It must be a wonderful place."

"Um, not quite." Tony solemnly explained that in his time there were crazy, incurable diseases that scared the hell out of everybody, there always seemed to be a war somewhere, and homelessness was a growing problem. Nearly everyone worried about overpopulation, using up all of the oil and other natural resources, and polluting the land, water, and the air.

"Seems like y'all spend more time and money entertaining yourselves instead of helping each other and solving your problems. Not much to look forward to." She looked Tony in the eye. "You know, I read some stories about the future, and Daddy always talks about it, and I dreamed about what it might be like. I used to feel bad that I might not live long enough to see everything that was to come. From what you say, I think I like it better right here and now." She stood. "Come on. The cot downstairs is ready for you to get some sleep. I'll put some water in the tub so you can take a bath, and I'll get you one of Daddy's nightgowns. Just leave your clothes on the floor, and I'll wash them for you."

"Um…thank you," Tony said sheepishly as he followed her out of the bathroom.

"You know what?" Ollie said without looking back. "You can keep your future."

Chapter 6

Sunday, July 27, 1919

9:35 a.m.

The Black Belt—Chicago, Illinois

Tony woke with a start. This was not his bedroom. Where the hell was he? He squinted as sunlight streamed in from a small window near the ceiling. A twinge of pain shot up his spine as he sat up on the cramped little bed and rubbed his eyes. When his head began to clear, he realized that he had done the impossible. He was 100-some years in the past, lying on a cot in the basement of Dr. Simmie Johnson's house. In his workshop, actually—the same room that would be Tony's workshop and lab in the 21st century.

He got up from the bed and walked across the room to examine the doctor's lab equipment. There were test tubes, all sorts of bulky electrical gear, and stacks of books, all looking like something out of an old Boris Karloff movie. A single bare electric bulb hung from the ceiling. *So, Dr. Johnson does have electricity,* he thought. He remembered reading that electricity was something of a luxury in this time, and not everyone would have it. At least he would be able to recharge the Chronocar's batteries if he ever had to.

On the table was what looked like a can capacitor, not unlike the ones he used in the Chronocar. It was about three inches tall and a couple of inches around. It had been sliced open as if someone was trying to figure out how it worked. An undamaged capacitor lay on the table next to it, with letters and numbers stamped on it indicating its specifications.

Behind him was a bookcase with several books on higher mathematics, physics, and chemistry. On the top shelf there was a blurry antique photograph of an old dark-skinned woman in an elaborate silver frame and a framed doctorate degree from Tuskegee Institute signed by Booker T. Washington and Dr. George Washington Carver. Next to that were two books held upright by fancy wooden bookends. One book was a King James Bible. The other was a copy of *The Principia* by Isaac Newton

"Tony!" Ollie's voice came from upstairs. "Breakfast is ready!"

On a table next to the cot were his clothes, clean and neatly folded. He pulled off the nightgown, put on his jeans and T-shirt, and made his way up the stairs.

The heavenly smell of bacon, eggs, and homemade biscuits greeted him when he stepped into the kitchen. Ollie stood at the big, black, silver-trimmed cast iron stove, stirring something. The kitchen was a big room, with a black-and-white checkerboard tiled floor and flowery wallpaper. There was a white porcelain sink near the stove with a single faucet, a flimsy curtain hiding the plumbing below. In the back of the room there was a potbellied coal-burning stove with a pipe that rose straight up 8 or 9 feet, turned 90 degrees, then disappeared into the wall near the ceiling. A curious wooden chest, about five feet tall with side-by-side doors and metal hinges, stood against the wall. A large heavy-looking wooden table and four sturdy wooden chairs were situated in the center of the room.

Ollie placed a plate of food on the table where he sat. She stood and watched as he tasted the fried eggs. They were delicious, like no other eggs he had ever had before. The biscuit was dense, fluffy, and dripping with rich, luscious butter. He took a bite of a thick slice of bacon.

"Ow!"

Ollie playfully slapped his arm. "You're not supposed to eat the rind, dummy!" She giggled.

"The rind?"

She showed him how to nibble the meat off the strip of tough skin along the edge of the bacon. "They don't have bacon where you come from?" She licked her lips.

"Yeah, we do, but it doesn't have a rind on it. And it's a lot thinner than this," he said, holding a piece up to the light. "The bacon I'm used to eating is so thin you could almost see through it." He took a sip of lemonade. "This lemonade is delicious."

"We always put a little honey in our lemonade. My father taught me that."

"Where is Dr. Johnson, by the way?" Tony asked.

"Daddy is upstairs asleep. He was up all night studying your time machine and such. I don't have to work today, so I thought I would try to be a good hostess and make sure you were comfortable."

"That's very thoughtful. Thanks. Where do you work?"

"Marshall Field's. In the millinery shop."

"What kind of shop?"

"You don't have millinery shops? Don't women wear hats in your time?" She sighed. "I'm not all that impressed with your future."

"I'm sure if a woman in my time wants a hat, she'd be able to find one," he laughed. "Look, I feel terrible about the damage and the mess I made when

I landed here yesterday. The least I can do is help you clean up the dust and everything."

"Daddy and I did all that while you were sleeping. It's all clean now. We even wiped as much dust as we could off your Chrono-thing."

"Now I feel even worse, but thank you." Tony laughed. "I want to go out and take a look around town. Do you want to come with me?" Ollie frowned. "I promise not to get into any trouble. You can be my guide."

"Well, okay, I guess," she responded. "Finish your breakfast and help me with the dishes first."

As he ate the last of his breakfast, he watched Ollie put the bowl with the fresh eggs and the paper-wrapped slab of bacon in the right side of the wooden cabinet, which was lined with metal on the inside.

"Won't that stuff spoil in there?" he asked.

"No, plenty of ice," she replied. She opened the left door and showed him a large, shiny cake of partly melted ice. She bent over and carefully removed a pan that was on the floor under the chest. It was nearly overflowing with water as she carried it gingerly to the sink and poured the water out. Then she placed it back under the chest. Ollie took the steaming tea kettle off the stove, poured hot water into a large pan on the counter next to the sink, and shaved little curls off a russet-colored bar of soap. Then she turned on the faucet and filled the sink with water from the tap.

Tony shook his head as she took his empty plate and glass to the sink. He watched with fascination as she rotated a little metal platform from under the sink that turned out to be a clever little seat. She sat and then dropped the utensils into the steamy water.

"I'll wash, you dry," she said, tossing a towel at him playfully.

He got up and stood at the counter, gazing at her. He found himself quite attracted to her. Typical, he thought, for him to develop feelings for a woman when he was only here for a short visit. A frilly white apron covered her calico sundress as she washed a glass, dipped it several times into the clear water, and handed it to him. He carefully wiped it dry inside and out.

"Just set it on the counter there," she directed. "You know, I guess I should apologize to you for yesterday. I wasn't very nice to you."

"Don't worry about it." Tony smiled as he dried a plate and placed it on the stack. "But you know, where I come from is really not all that bad."

She smiled timidly while she played absent-mindedly in the soapy water. "So, tell me something good about your time."

"Well, we usually don't do dishes like this in my house," Tony chuckled.

"You have servants?"

"No," he said. "But we do have a dishwasher."

"Whether they are washing dishes or washing clothes, they're still servants."

"No, I mean we have a machine that washes the dishes, and one to wash the clothes."

"I've seen clothes-washing machines," Ollie said pensively. "Daddy said we might get one. But how can a machine wash dishes without breaking them?"

Tony shrugged.

"Probably gets the dishes cleaner," she said.

"Yeah, but this is much more fun." Tony could not believe he had said that.

"I see," Ollie said seriously. "But some people have servants, don't they? I mean like cooks, valets, and maids?"

"Some people do."

"Are they…?" She stopped and dried her hands on her apron. "Are the servants all colored?"

Tony smiled again. "In my time we don't call ourselves 'colored.' We prefer to use the term 'black.'"

"Black? You don't find that a little insulting?"

"No."

"Okay…" she spoke with a little hesitation, "are all of the servants in your time…'black'?"

"Not all of them. There are rich black people with white servants. I mean, times are…different. It will get worse before it gets better, but it will get better. As a matter of fact, in 2008, a black man will be elected President of the United States!"

Ollie glared at him open-mouthed.

"And he was re-elected in 2012 and was—is—still serving in 2015."

Ollie pouted. "Our people don't have much to hope for here and now. You're probably not going to like 1919 very much."

"Oh, I don't know. I kind of like it so far."

Ollie covered her face with one hand and looked away. "I think we should get going," she tittered.

⎯⎯⎯◆◇◆⎯⎯⎯

They stepped out into the summer heat. Ollie's dress fluttered in the breeze, clinging to her body, the long skirt with ruffles at the bottom barely covering the black lace-up shoes that hid her ankles. A wide-brimmed straw hat kept the sun off her face. Tony had been concerned about his clothes, but

49

Ollie assured him that many men walked around in T-shirts, blue jeans, and canvas shoes in the summer, although the image on his shirt and the color of his shoes might attract some attention.

"What is that thing on your shirt, anyway?" Ollie said as they stood in front of the house.

"Spiderman. He is a character from a comic book."

"A comic? You mean like Krazy Kat?"

"I suppose so. Don't you have a purse or something?" Tony asked.

"A purse? No. Gets in the way. I just sewed pockets into my skirts and dresses." She pulled a little clutch bag from a pocket. "I carry my money and stuff in here."

Tony grinned. "You're just full of surprises, aren't you?"

"Just being practical. So, let's see, what should I show you first?" Ollie wondered aloud as she peered up and down the street.

"I know exactly where I want to go," Tony said, then took her by the hand. He led her south on Vincennes Street, past the well-kept homes with healthy, young trees along the curb. They turned right at 47th Street, and Tony stopped and gawked. He was not sure what he had expected, but it certainly wasn't this. It almost looked the same as in his time. The buildings were not quite as rundown, but they still looked old and dingy. Trash danced across the pavement in the wind. The people almost seemed the same, just dressed differently.

He stopped to take a photo and noticed a man glaring at him. He put the phone away and quietly led Ollie down the street. He actually recognized some of the shops they passed. They were not as brightly lit, and the windows were covered with paper signs on the inside. But he knew this little grocery store would be a pawnshop, and the barbershop would still be a barbershop.

"Are you all right?" Ollie asked.

"I walked up and down this street a lot in my time. I guess I thought it would look different now."

"You mean it looks the same?"

"Almost." He looked to the west. "What the hell? Is that what I think it is down there?" He pointed at the metal bridge that crossed over the street several blocks ahead.

"You mean the elevated? You have elevated trains?"

"Not only do we have them," Tony laughed, "but we have that same one! I mean, yeah, our trains are newer and the stations are different, but it's the same system. I had no idea it was that old. Goes downtown, right?"

"Yes." Ollie looked puzzled. "You mean to tell me that a century from

50

now they couldn't do any better than the elevated for transportation?"

"Look at it this way," Tony said with a grin. "It was so well-built that it lasted that long."

"It used to be run with steam engines, but now it is all electrified. What do your trains run on?"

"Electricity," Tony said flatly.

"Humph." Ollie pulled away from him. "Hasn't there been *any* advancement between now and then?"

"We got rid of those." He gestured toward the trolley car that rumbled by.

"What do you have instead?"

"Busses and cars."

"Flying cars?"

"No." Tony was starting to get a little annoyed. "Our cars are sleeker and faster, but they still use wheels. You saw the pictures."

"Yes, but they are still just cars. And busses. And trains," she said.

"Okay, I think I've seen enough for now," Tony muttered.

"I did it again, didn't I? I'm sorry." Ollie sighed.

"Not your fault," he said. "A lot of what you're saying is true. I just never thought of it that way. A lot of things didn't change all that much."

Ollie looked at him sympathetically and slid her arm under his. He smiled weakly, enjoying being so close to her as they headed back toward the house. He noticed that people here seemed more relaxed. No iPods, no smartphones, no Bluetooth headsets. Everyone strolled casually along the sidewalks with no real sense of urgency, no need to rush anywhere. In the distance, he saw what looked like factories spewing thick, black smoke into the air. Yet above it all, the sky was extremely clear, just a few puffy clouds. No airplanes or vapor trails, just a blimp floating lazily in the sky. There was also very little in the way of noise. Occasionally, he'd hear the rattle of an automobile, the clanging of a streetcar bell, or the neighing of a horse somewhere. He commented on how little traffic there was, and Ollie explained that it was a Sunday morning, and things would not get busy until much later in the day. It was mostly quiet save for chirping birds and the wind rustling through trees. He took a few pictures, shooting from the hip so no one would see.

He tried to be as nonchalant as possible; still, folks stared at him. He wasn't exactly dressed like a typical 1919 Chicagoan. The T-shirt and blue jeans weren't too out of place; it was the Spiderman image and the bright red gym shoes that seemed to attract attention.

They arrived back at the house. Ollie removed her hat, placed it on the rocking chair on the porch, and fluffed her hair.

"Hey, baby!" A tall, skinny, rather good-looking young black man in a bright blue suit came jogging across the street. "Ollie! How you doin'? I ain't seen you since... Who this?"

Tony quickly jammed his phone into his pocket.

"Jojo," Ollie groaned. "What do you want?"

"You know what I want, baby."

Tony cleared his throat loudly.

"Who *is* this?" Jojo insisted.

"This is Tony. He is visiting us from, uh...Africa."

Tony spoke in the best African accent he could muster. "I am her cousin."

Jojo gave Tony the once-over. "Those some sissy-looking clothes, son. Is that how they dress over in Africa? I mean, I thought you Africans wore grass drawers and beads..."

"What do you want, Jojo?" Ollie interrupted.

"I want to know why you don't come around no more, baby."

"Jojo, now, I told you about that. You're nasty. I don't like that."

"I be good, I promise."

Tony swallowed hard. "I think you should leave her alone," he said, the accent getting a little thin.

"Back off, boy," Jojo growled. "I'm talkin' to the lady."

"You are *not* talking to me!" Ollie shot back.

"Aw, baby!"

"All right, that's enough." Tony wondered how he was going to back up his bravado. Fighting was not exactly his strong suit. "I think you should just leave now."

"Look, you little African punk..." Jojo grabbed Tony by the front of his shirt.

In what seemed like slow motion, Ollie took Jojo by the shoulder and, catching him off balance, spun him around. An instant later her fist connected with his face, and Jojo fell to the ground.

"What you do that for?" Jojo cried as he slowly got to his feet, rubbing his cheek. "I wasn't gonna hurt him!"

"You fool. I told you where he was from. Don't you know nothing about Africans? He can kill you with that hoodoo-voodoo stuff! Now, you get your silly self out of here," Ollie yelled. "Go on!"

"Okay, all right. You didn't have to hit me!" Jojo made his way back across the street, still rubbing his jaw. "Ollie! You wanna go to the show on Friday?" he shouted.

Ollie picked up a stone and pitched it with remarkable precision. Jojo ducked just in time, shrugged, and walked on.

Ollie's expression changed from fury to a demure smile. "Are you okay?" she asked.

"Me? I'm fine," Tony said, looking at his feet.

"I was just preventing a fight," Ollie said. She reached over and straightened his shirt. "Jojo's the sissy. If a girl like me can beat him up, then you would have knocked him out."

Tony wanted to believe her. He knew he wasn't very tough-looking and no threat to the likes of Jojo. He had spent most of his formative years doing all he could to avoid fights.

Ollie took his hand. "I'm sorry. I know how to handle Jojo. You would have gotten into a fight for nothing."

"Uh-huh," Tony sighed.

"Come on, we are going to have to do something about your clothes," she said. "That might be all right in your time, but here? Well, you heard what Jojo called you. I know where you can get some better clothes."

"The millinery shop?"

Ollie laughed. "No, dummy! A haberdasher!" She retrieved her hat and carefully placed it on her head.

"Haberdasher? That's like a men's clothing store, right?"

"Right. It belongs to a white boy named Bobby McNab, who sells to colored people. Matter of fact, you'll probably get a real good deal."

"Why?"

"Well, he kinda likes me."

They walked back to 47th Street and headed east. McNab's was a well-kept little tailor's shop near Cottage Grove in the middle of the Black Belt. Inside, a buff young Irishman with slick, combed-back black hair stood behind the counter counting money, his shirt unbuttoned just enough to show a tuft of chest hair. Tony's heart sank. This was a rather handsome young white man. Big and macho. He wondered how Ollie felt about him. Little chimes tinkled as they entered, startling the Irishman, who quickly put his money away.

"Oh, hello, Ollie!" His blue eyes sparkled. "What brings you here?"

"Hello, Bobby." Ollie beamed an irresistible smile. "My friend here needs a new suit of clothes."

McNab sniggered. "Where did he get these? I mean, he is one funny-looking…"

"Bobby!" Ollie chastised. "This is Tony. He is the son of a dear friend of my father's. He came all the way from Africa to visit us. Don't you go

53

insulting him now."

"Oh, I'm sorry. Is that the way they dress over there?"

"Sometimes," Tony answered, wishing Ollie would be a little more consistent with her story.

"What is that on your shirt?"

"Hoodoo voodoo," Tony said flatly.

"That is an African god, right, Tony?" Ollie said.

"Yes, the Spider King," Tony said soberly.

"Do say!" McNab raised an eyebrow. "Well, what did you have in mind?"

"Oh, a nice summer suit, I think," Ollie said.

McNab pulled a tape measure from his shirt pocket and gestured to Tony. "Step over here." He carefully measured Tony, winking and grinning at Ollie the whole time, who giggled in return. Tony soon realized that he just didn't like the attention McNab was giving her nor did he like how she was responding. She was probably playing along with him to get a good deal on the suit, he reminded himself, and tried to dismiss it. McNab explained that it usually took a few days to fit a man properly with one of his fine garments, but it seemed that Tony's measurements were very close to one of the suits on the rack. It would just take a few minutes to make alterations.

The big Irishman then had Tony try on a suit made of some lightweight material. McNab tucked and pinned, once jabbing Tony in the thigh in what he thought was not altogether an accident. McNab then took the clothes to a room in the back. Tony chuckled as he watched this huge figure of a man bend over a pedal-operated sewing machine.

Tony put on the altered suit, transferring his wallet and phone from his old clothes. It was not bad, actually. Apparently, the best in style for the times. Brown trousers, a matching suit coat, and a white button-down shirt with a rather wide red-striped tie. He hurried out of the dressing room when he heard the two of them laughing.

"How do I look?"

"Very handsome!" Ollie said.

"A hell of a lot better than when you came in here," the big Irishman laughed. "But you're still going to have to do something about those funny-looking shoes."

"Now, Bobby, cut that out," Ollie said seriously. "We'll find a cobbler next."

"My cousin Donnie has a cobbler's shop up on Wells Street," McNab said.

"Now, you know colored people can't go up in that neighborhood," Ollie reminded him.

"Oh, yeah. Well, could you use a nice hat maybe?"

Tony followed McNab's gesture to a stack of stiff-looking yellow straw hats with brightly colored bands and visualized Vaudeville clowns prancing around on a stage. "Ah, no thank you."

McNab shrugged. "Usually, that suit would cost almost 30 dollars, but since you're a friend of Ollie's, I'll give it to you for twenty-five."

"Twenty-five dollars? Sure, just a minute." *I'll teach this Mr. Bobby McNab a little lesson,* Tony thought with a grin as he produced a crisp, new fifty-dollar bill from his wallet.

"Damn! I didn't know Africans had this kind of money," McNab exclaimed as he opened the cash drawer. "I should have change… Hey!" McNab slammed the fifty on the counter and laid a twenty-dollar bill next to it. "What the hell you tryin' to pull?" Tony's money was a full half-inch smaller in size, and the lettering and color were markedly different.

"Tony!" Ollie snatched the fifty off the counter. "I told you that you can't use that money here." She reached into her pocket and gave the fuming McNab some cash from her little purse. "My credit is still good here for the rest, right?" Ollie smiled at McNab.

"Always," McNab muttered as he stuffed the bills in the drawer. "What the hell was that all about, anyway?"

"The money that the United States makes in other countries is different from the money we use here," Ollie explained. "Thank you, Bobby," she said sweetly, then took Tony's arm and led him outside.

"That was close," Tony said as they stepped out onto the sidewalk. "I guess I didn't think about differences in the money."

Ollie examined the bill. "Good thing he didn't see the date!" She gave him the fifty back and rustled through her purse. "Here, take this." She handed him some coins.

"What's this for?"

"Can't use your money," she smiled as she slipped her hand around his arm. "You're going to need something to buy me a cherry Coca Cola at Walgreens!"

They walked several blocks west to South Parkway. For a nickel each, they rode the noisy, uncomfortable trolley up north to 35th Street. Tony couldn't help but grin when he saw the old-fashioned Walgreens drugstore on the corner. He supposed it was as good as any other place to get a bottle of soda.

55

It was much cooler inside the store thanks to the ceiling fans that were driven by a network of belts. Naked electric bulbs offered some dim lighting. The store was quite large with a lot of open floor space. Shelves displaying colorful bottles and boxes lined the walls. Customers, some white, some black, spoke to the white clerks in white jackets that stood behind the counters. This surprised Tony a little, since his research seemed to suggest some tension between the races in this time. He made a mental note to ask Ollie about that later. In the back of the room there was a bar made of dark polished wood with a half-dozen red padded leather stools atop shiny metal bases. Ollie guided him to the bar where there were glasses, dishes, and large bottles containing colored liquids in a huge cupboard. Behind the bar stood a young white man with a white coat, bright red tie, and flaming red hair that peeked out from under his white paper hat.

"Hey, Ollie." The man smiled.

Is there any good-looking white boy she doesn't know? Tony wondered to himself, a little surprised at his jealousy.

"Hi, Mickey," Ollie said, carefully adjusting her dress as she sat on one of the stools. "This is my cousin Anthony."

"Hey there, Anthony," Mickey said.

"Hey," Tony replied flatly.

"What can I get you two?"

"I would just love a cherry Coca Cola," Ollie said.

"Alrighty! And you, Anthony?"

"Uh, just a regular Coke," Tony said.

"What did you call it?" Mickey grinned. "A 'Coke'? That's funny!" He took a small glass from the shelf behind him. Tony watched as he tossed the glass from one hand to the other, and with more than a little flair, poured a dark brown syrup from a bottle into the glass. Mickey took another bottle and poured some red liquid on top of the dark syrup. Then he held it under a shiny, long-necked faucet. He pulled a lever, snapping it back and forth as fizzy water bubbled into the little glass. He placed the drink on the bar in front of Ollie.

"Mmmm," she purred after taking a sip.

Mickey mixed Tony's regular Coca Cola. Tony took a swig. It was cold and delicious. He drank it down. "That was good. Can I have another one…a large this time?"

"Only one size." Mickey took another little glass from the shelf and poured syrup into it.

"You're not supposed to gulp it down like that." Ollie laughed.

"Aren't you popular?" Tony said softly. "First McNab and now this guy?"

"I'm just a friendly kinda girl. Tony Carpenter, you jealous?" She giggled.

Tony flushed. "Uh, no. I just thought that, uh, that white people and colored people didn't get along so well with each other in this time, that's all."

"Well, Bobby makes all of Daddy's suits, and me and my friends come here for Coca Colas all the time. I mean, some white people are nice. Look around the store. White people and colored people getting along okay. There's even a colored clerk who works here a couple of nights a week."

"Sure you don't want a flavored Coca Cola?" Mickey interrupted. "I have cherry, lemon, lime, vanilla, and licorice."

"Regular is fine," Tony said. Mickey finished mixing the drink. Tony sipped the soda as he quietly listened to the small talk between Ollie and Mickey. Apparently, Mickey had been at the beach with some dude named Tommy Haynes, who'd picked up a fish that had washed ashore and hit Mickey in the face with it.

Mickey and Ollie laughed. Tony faked amusement and swallowed the last of the soda.

"You want another one?" Mickey asked him.

"No thanks," Tony said as he reached for the money in his pocket.

A tremendous crash in the front of the store made them jump. Tony turned just in time to see one of the large glass windows come crashing down. Outside, two young white men were yelling, "Nigger lovers! Got no business serving niggers! We ought to burn this damned place down!" Patrons and staff inside the store stood in horror as the offenders hopped in a car and drove away.

"Son of a bitch!" Mickey slapped the counter. "I am so sorry, folks. Crazy people been causing trouble all week. Ollie, why don't you and your cousin come this way. I'll let you out back. It will be safer."

"How much do I owe you?" Tony asked.

"Don't you worry about that, just come on." Mickey lifted part of the counter up, and they followed him through a stock room to the back. "I swear, I don't know what is wrong with some people." He shook his head as he led them to a door that opened onto an alley. "You should be fine if you leave this way."

"Thank you, Mickey." Ollie gave him a peck on the cheek. His face turned nearly as red as his tie.

"You two be careful and go right home!" Mickey yelled as they started down the alley. "You look out for her, you hear?"

"I will, thanks," Tony called back.

As they walked down the alley, Ollie asked, "Does this kind of stuff happen in your time?"

Tony sighed. "Sort of. I mean, yes, I guess it does. Although this is the first time that I have personally ever experienced it. The truth is, up until now I had only seen it in the news. Never happens where I live. I mean, my parents told me about stuff that happened to them when they were younger, but people get along a little better in my time, I think."

"Part of our everyday life," Ollie said, shaking. "Seems like it's a little worse this summer."

He took her by the arm. "I think we better go straight home."

Chapter 7

Tony and Ollie were sitting at the kitchen table sipping honey lemonade when Dr. Johnson walked in.

"And where were you two this afternoon?" he said, eyeing Tony's new clothes.

"We went shopping." Ollie grinned.

"Yes, I bought… I mean, Ollie bought these clothes so I would be a little less conspicuous." Tony chuckled. "You should have heard what people were calling me."

"If they called you a fool, they were right. Where did you go?"

"Bobby McNab's," Ollie said. "He gave it to us at a good price, too."

"Oh, my Lord!" Dr. Johnson shook his head.

"What's the matter?" Tony asked.

"What's the matter?" The doctor sat down at the kitchen table. "Son, you can't just walk around and do whatever you please in this time. That is an extremely dangerous thing to do." He turned to Ollie. "I thought I asked you to look after him."

"It's not her fault, sir. Besides, all we did was a little sightseeing." Tony shrugged.

"Don't you realize that anything you do here, *anything* you do, could have catastrophic results?"

Tony smiled. Dr. Johnson was obviously overreacting. "As long as folks don't know anything about me, as long as no one else learns where I've come from, there shouldn't be a problem."

"Where do you think that McNab boy thought you were from dressed the way you were?"

"From Africa!" Ollie chimed in. "I told him Tony was from Africa, and he believed it."

Dr. Johnson sighed. "Please leave us, Ollie."

"But, Daddy…"

"I said leave us, please!"

Ollie's face twisted into a pout. Then she got up from the table and stomped out of the room.

Dr. Johnson sighed. "Look, son, your very presence here is dangerous. Your chance meeting with someone could somehow result in them doing something—or not doing something—they were or were not supposed to do. The possibilities are endless. It is probably already too late; you may have already changed history significantly!"

"All we did was look around and buy some clothes." Tony decided not to mention the trip to the drugstore. "That's all we did."

"You did much more than that!" the doctor shouted as he stood up. "You conversed with people! You talked to McNab! What happened to your old clothes?"

Tony's spine tingled. They left his old clothes at McNab's shop. "I'm sure McNab has thrown them out."

Dr. Johnson stomped over to the counter and slammed his fist down. "Dammit, boy! You have no idea what you are doing!"

Tony took a deep breath. The doctor had obviously forgotten the details of his own theory. He reminded the doctor of his own writings which stated that a time traveler would be safe in any time other than his own, because that time was not his own. The timeline from July 1919 to July 2015 was fixed. It had all already happened, and it could not be changed. Nothing could happen to the traveler.

The doctor hovered over Tony and pointed a finger in his face. "You were protected while you were within the Tesla field. You would have been safe no matter what, because you and the Chronocar would still physically be in your time; you were carrying a bit of 2015 with you inside. Once you switched the field off, you became a part of this time. As long as you are here, you are as vulnerable as the rest of us. And your actions here can change what happens in the future."

"No, Doctor! I am part of 2015. I always will be. I could not be here in 1919 if 2015 didn't still exist. And 2015 cannot exist without me, because I am a part of that time." Tony paused for a moment, then continued. "I can't make any significant changes. I can't do anything that could change 2015, because 2015 and everything about it already exists. It still exists, and I can't change what has already happened. So, I can't hurt anybody, and nothing can harm me."

Suddenly, Dr. Johnson smacked Tony across the face.

"What the hell is wrong with you?" Tony said as he rubbed his stinging cheek.

"Did that hurt?" Dr. Johnson said.

"Damn right it hurt!"

"Son, if you can hurt, then you can bleed. And if you can bleed, you can die. Don't ever forget that!"

Tony stood dumbfounded as the doctor stormed out of the kitchen.

Chapter 8

Larry Hawkins tugged at the corner of the blanket, then stuck his head out into the hallway. "Mama, can I go outside now?"

"Let me see that bed first!" Larry's mother stepped into his bedroom and examined his bed. The pillow was crooked, and the blankets were uneven. "You can go out, but you stay nearby on this block, you hear me?"

"Okay, Mama." Larry ran past her.

"Larry," she called, placing her hands on her hips. "You better come back here and give your mama some sugar."

Larry turned and gave her a kiss on the cheek. Then he darted out the door, down the stairs, and into the brutal midsummer sun. Larry could not have guessed what the temperature was. He just knew that it was hot. Damn hot. He stood in the doorway, taking advantage of the small shade it offered, looking for his best friend, Pookie.

Now, Pookie was fun. He knew all kinds of ways to have a good time. Mama would beat him silly if she knew some of the things he and Pookie had done. Like the time they made a dummy out of some old clothes stuffed with rags and threw it in front of speeding cars. It was better that she didn't know. Mothers could never understand what it meant to be an 11-year-old boy.

Larry had just stepped onto the hot sidewalk when he heard the sound of little metal wheels on the cobblestone pavement in the distance. There, in the middle of Wentworth Avenue, was Pookie riding his homemade scooter—an old two-by-four with an orange crate nailed to it and wheels from somebody's discarded roller skates. He was holding the back of a motorcar as it sped down the street.

"Pookie!"

Pookie let go of the car and turned toward him, weaving to miss a horse and wagon. He was still going pretty fast. Pookie jumped from the scooter just as it struck the curb. He landed on a pile of trash and rolled over onto the sidewalk. The scooter flew into the air and crashed through a plate glass window. By the time the store owner could come out to investigate, Larry and Pookie were already around the corner, running like crazy. When they felt they had covered a safe distance, they stopped and sat down on the curb and laughed.

"Man, I thought you was gonna die!" Larry said as he wiped the sweat from his forehead with the bottom of his shirt.

"Me, too!" Pookie panted. "I couldn't stop that damn thang! You see it go through that window? *Whooo-bang!*"

They sat quietly for a few minutes watching the traffic go by. "Damn, it's hot," Larry said, thinking that if his mama ever heard him cuss like that, she would whip him good.

"Then let's go swimmin'."

"Naw, man." Larry recalled the last time they went swimming near some factories. It was a much cooler day, and Pookie said he knew of a place where the water was warm. The water was indeed warm, especially where it poured out of the big pipe that protruded from one of the buildings. They splashed and played in the shallow water for almost two hours. It was great fun until Larry noticed that his skin was changing color. When they got out of the water and dried off, they were both almost as pale as white boys. Scared the hell out of him and his mother, who fretted something awful until it finally wore off a day and a half later. Then she beat him to within an inch of his life with a piece of clothesline. No, Larry didn't want to go swimming.

"Aw, man, I ain't talkin' about that place we went to last time," Pookie said. "Don't nobody want to go swimmin' in hot water today. I mean the beach over on 29th Street."

Now, that sounded like fun. "How we gonna get there?" Larry asked.

"Come on!"

The beach was a long way off, and they didn't have money to ride the streetcar. So, they stood at the corner and waited for a means of transportation. It soon appeared. A half-empty produce truck. As the truck slowed to turn the corner, the two boys jumped on. They hid among the crates of fruits and vegetables, helping themselves to a couple of juicy apples. Each time the truck stopped, they would jump off and hide while the driver unloaded his deliveries. At State Street they hopped off while the truck paused at a stop sign. Then they walked to the lakefront.

An unwritten law decreed that the beach south of 29th Street was for whites only. To the north, Negroes could swim. There was even a Negro lifeguard. Between the two was a sort of no-man's land, a small stretch of sand that was a little dirtier than the other beaches and partly obstructed by an old pier.

"Hey, look!" Pookie spotted a homemade raft made with scrap wood hidden under the pier.

Larry grinned. They had no bathing suits, and Larry knew that if his clothes were wet or even looked like they had been wet, Mama would whip his ass. So, they stripped naked. They waded in and treaded clumsily in the water as they untied the raft. Neither boy was much of a swimmer. So, they clung tightly to the raft and paddled into the lake.

The cool water felt wonderful. And when it got too cold, they would climb onto the raft for a little sun.

"Let's go out a little further," Pookie said as he slid back into the water.

"I don't know. We're pretty far out now," Larry said, looking at what seemed like a mile of water between them and the shore.

"Aw, man, don't be no scaredy cat. We stay near the wall," Pookie said, pointing to the breakwater that jutted out into the lake a hundred feet away.

"Okay…" Larry said, feeling a little chill as he got back into the water. The beaches were full of people, but none of them ventured anywhere near the forbidden zone—except for one white man in a blue shirt. He seemed to be staring at them from the breakwater. The boys had seen him but paid little attention.

"What was that?" Larry said. "Did you hear somethin'?"

"What?" Pookie asked. There was another splash, and the boys turned. The man on the breakwater was laughing. He picked up a large stone and threw it at them. They ducked under the raft as the stone bounced off the wood.

"Why he doin' that, Pookie?" Larry asked. All the white people he knew were nice, like his teacher and the nurse at the clinic. He could not understand why a white person was trying to hurt them.

"I don't know. My mama say white people is crazy. Look out!" Pookie ducked as another stone splashed near him.

"This fool can't even throw!" Pookie chuckled. They made faces at the man, easily dodging his missiles.

After a couple of minutes, Larry didn't think it was funny anymore. "Let's get outta here, Pookie."

Pookie agreed, and he got behind the raft and started paddling back toward the pier.

"Pookie, look out!" Larry yelled as he saw a piece of red brick come flying through the air. It struck Pookie on the forehead. His body went limp, and he slipped into the water.

"Pookie! Where you at?" Larry pulled himself around to the other side of the raft and searched the surface of the water. Something grabbed at his foot. He panicked and instinctively kicked it away. Then he climbed onto the raft, never considering that it might have been Pookie reaching for help. He saw the man in the blue shirt running away on the breakwater.

Larry paddled the raft to the shore as quickly as he could. Ignoring his clothes lying in the sand, he ran north to the Negro beach. He made his way through the crowds to the big, muscular lifeguard who was standing next to his high chair talking to a couple of young women.

"Mistah!" Larry said, his lungs gulping air.

The lifeguard looked down at him, then continued his conversation with the women.

Larry tugged on the lifeguard's bathing suit. "Mistah lifeguard! He drownin'!"

"Go put some clothes on, boy!" the lifeguard scowled at him.

"It's Pookie! He's drownin'!"

"Who's drownin'? Where?"

Larry pointed toward the old pier. The lifeguard took off, kicking up sand and drawing attention as he ran. Dozens of curious people trotted after him. When he reached the breakwater, the lifeguard dived in, swimming underwater for long seconds. Larry stood on the beach watching the water, speechless. He imagined Pookie floating on the water, probably just knocked out by the brick. *He will be all right,* he thought nervously. *The lifeguard will save him.* Folks stood on the beach and the breakwater, black people and white people together, momentarily wrapped up in the drama. The lifeguard came up for air. "Where was he, boy?"

"Right where you is!" Larry pointed.

He dove again. Moments stretched on for eternity as Larry stood there helplessly in the scorching sun, the sand burning his feet.

Suddenly, the lifeguard's head bobbed out of the water, and he gulped for air. "I got him," he shouted. The lifeguard swam laboriously to the shore, pulling Pookie's limp body onto the beach.

Larry ran over and kneeled next to his friend. "Pookie! You okay? Say somethin', Pookie!" Larry wailed. His eyes filled with tears.

"He's not going to be saying anything anymore," the lifeguard said as he looked over the body. "What happened here?" He rubbed the nasty-looking knot on Pookie's forehead.

Larry stared at his motionless friend, lying there with his eyes closed and a strange, peaceful look on his face. Somehow it didn't seem right for him to be lying there naked. He looked around for Pookie's clothes.

"I asked you what happened, boy," the lifeguard said again.

Larry blinked. "A man—a white man—was throwin' rocks at us. He threw a piece of brick and hit Pookie on the head. That's when he went in the water."

"What you say?" a big black man in a T-shirt thundered. "You say a white man did this? Was you throwin' rocks at him?"

"We wasn't doin' nothin'! We just swimmin'!"

"On the white beach!" a pale woman called out. "They had no business there!"

"That don't give nobody no cause to throw rocks at the child!" a black woman chimed in. "He was only a little boy. Maybe he didn't know no better."

"Damn niggers got to remember to keep in your place, that's all!" came another voice from the crowd.

"Just a minute!" the lifeguard yelled. "Let's keep calm now!"

"Who the hell do you think you're talking to, nigger?"

"Who you callin' a 'nigger'?" the lifeguard growled, scanning the group of angry whites for the man who insulted him.

"Watch it, boy!" an old white man in the front shouted.

A stone flew out from the crowd and struck the lifeguard on the leg.

"Son of a bitch!" He picked up the rock and flung it back. A little white girl screamed when it grazed her head.

"Goddamned nigger! You hit my little girl!" The incensed father charged from the mob and tackled the lifeguard to the ground.

They rolled around in the sand while cheers and jeers came from the opposing hordes: whites on one side, blacks on the other. There was the loud report of a gun—or it could have been a firecracker—and the black people responded by charging into the crowd of whites. Fists, sticks, and stones flew as years of pent-up rage and frustration erupted. Little Larry watched the scene unfold, naked and terrified. A group of white men relentlessly beat on a young black man, his face covered in blood. A white man struck a small black girl so hard she fell to the ground. A second later, a black woman was beating the man senseless. Both groups were in combat, trying to kill each other, and Larry could not understand why.

"Y'all stop that fightin'!" he screamed as tears burned his eyes. "Stop it!" He was still on his knees next to Pookie, shaking his lifeless body. "Get up, Pookie! Please! Let's go home! Please get up, Pookie!"

There was a gunshot. Then another. The mobs fell silent while two white policemen fought their way through the crowd. "Break it up!" one of them yelled in a thick Irish brogue. "Now, what the devil is goin' on here?"

The lifeguard, face bloodied, tried to explain the situation. The big Irish cop listened quietly, shaking his head, while his young partner stood nervously watching the crowd.

"All right, all right, there's nothin' more to see here," the Irish cop said, waving his arms at the mobs. "You all go home now!" He turned to his partner and said, "Billy, disperse this crowd, son."

"You heard him," Billy shouted in a shaky, high-pitched voice. "Go on now!"

Mumbled threats and insults grumbled through the crowd as the mob started to break up. Blacks headed north and whites headed south.

"Did ya see the man who did it, son?" the Irish cop asked Larry.

"Yes, suh. It was a white man," Larry said meekly.

The Irish cop sighed loudly.

Larry looked toward the people along the beach. Battle lines had already been drawn; epithets and empty bottles were being hurled back and forth. Then he saw him—the man who had thrown the brick that killed Pookie.

"Mistah police! That's him!"

"What?" the Irish cop said.

"That man over there with the blue shirt! He the one throwin' the rocks!"

"Shut up, ya little nigger!" the man in the blue shirt yelled. "He had no business over there!"

"Son of a bitch!" the lifeguard exclaimed, charging the man in the blue shirt. He had him on the ground in an instant. Billy ran up to the two men and struck the lifeguard on the skull with his nightstick. The man in the blue shirt stood up and brushed the sand off his clothes as the lifeguard's limp body lay in the sand.

Still naked and blinded by tears, Larry started running. Away from the angry mob, away from the hatred, away from the fighting…

Chapter 9

Sunday, July 27, 1919

6:05 p.m.

Tony was trying to clean the sticky, dried-up soda that covered everything in the Chronocar. He was using a spray bottle of all-purpose cleaner he had stashed in the drawer under the console and the remainder of the paper towels. While scrubbing all of the important surfaces, like the keyboard and monitor, he thought about the doctor's words earlier that day. Tony just could not see how his presence in 1919 could be all that dangerous. If 2015 still existed, then the timeline was basically fixed. It would have to be. It would be like a video file or a piece of film, just as Tony had explained to Jimmy. Editing a piece in the middle was not going to alter what was at the end. Okay, maybe he would cause some minor changes; McNab would now have a story to tell his friends about Ollie's weird African visitor, and Mickey had a chance to be something of a hero. So what? How could that have a significant effect on the future? Tony figured that after he returned to his time, Ollie would just tell them he went back home to Africa or wherever, and that would be the end of it. Dr. Johnson was worrying about nothing.

Still, he decided that once he got the machine all cleaned up, he would go back home in the morning. Just to be sure. Once he confirmed that nothing had changed, he could come back to 1919 and prove to Dr. Johnson he was wrong. Then he could take the Chronocar to visit other times and places. Maybe he could even talk Ollie into coming with him.

"Can I help?"

Tony nearly jumped out of his skin when he heard Ollie's voice. "God! Don't do that!" he said with a half-smile.

"I'm sorry. I didn't mean to startle you," Ollie replied. She was wearing an apron, and her hair was tied up with some kind of scarf. She held a bucket of steaming soapy water. "I came to help you clean up the mess."

"Thanks," he said, smiling. "But I already cleaned up most of it. And it wouldn't be a good idea to bring that water in here."

"Oh!" she gasped, and carefully placed the bucket on the floor. "Is there any way I can help?"

"Well, you can help by keeping me company."

Ollie nodded her head, then stepped into the Chronocar. She sat on the floor, pulled the scarf off her head, and fluffed her hair. She wrapped her arms around her knees and watched as Tony worked on the computer and explained the screen displays.

"This," he said as he entered a date, "is the destination setting. Whatever date I type here is where the Chronocar will take me."

"July 27, 2015. What's 18:00?"

"Six o'clock in the evening. About four hours after I left, actually. There should be someone there waiting for me."

"Your...girlfriend?" Ollie spoke softly.

Tony chuckled. "I don't have a girlfriend. I don't think any girl would want to hang around with a geek like me."

"A what?"

"I don't have a girlfriend. My buddy Jimmy is waiting for me." Tony looked into her lovely, dark eyes. Why couldn't he find a woman in his time who was more like Ollie? All the girls he'd ever known always seemed to have some hidden agenda. They were more interested in how a guy dressed, what kind of car he drove, or if he had money. Ollie was sweet and sincere. She played no games and had nothing to hide.

"I see." She looked him in the eye. "So, tell me how this thing works. You put in the date, then what?"

"Has your father told you anything about time travel?"

"He said that he had published some theories years ago and that one day someone from the future might figure it out and come to see us. I guess I never thought it would really happen...or that it would be someone like you."

Tony felt his face flush as he attempted to explain the process to her. After the destination date was entered into the computer, the Tesla field engaged. He explained how the Tesla field was a kind of invisible electromagnetic bubble that surrounded the Chronocar, protecting anyone inside from the changing times outside. It also worked as a kind of propeller to move the Chronocar through time.

"So, if we were to go back in time now," she asked, "what would we see out of the window? Would our house disappear when we passed the time it was built?"

"You would see outer space," Tony said. He explained the concept of transposition, trying to keep it as simple as possible. Once the time trip started the time machine would instantly be transposed, or moved, to a different point in space. It could be thousands or even millions of miles away, and whatever was there would transpose back to Earth.

"What? I don't understand that part," Ollie said.

"If the Chronocar were to transpose into, say, an ocean," Tony said, "then an equal volume of ocean water would appear here where the Chronocar was. The Chronocar and the water would simply switch places."

"So, the Chronocar would disappear, and a 10-foot ball of water would appear in its place?" Ollie knitted her brows. "But what if you transposed inside the sun?"

Tony felt a knot in his stomach as he pondered the answer. "Then a piece of the sun the size of the Chronocar would appear here."

"And you would be burned up!"

"No, I wouldn't. The Tesla field is a time barrier. Nothing, not even the heat of the sun, could penetrate it."

"But it could burn up the Earth. You would have to be very careful," Ollie said.

Tony swallowed hard. Transposition was a natural, uncontrollable side effect of time travel. He had no control over it nor any way of knowing for sure where he might transpose to during a time journey. He decided not to mention that.

"So, how does it know where to go when the time trip is over?"

"The computer keeps track of all that," Tony explained. "It figures out where the Earth will be when the Chronocar reaches its destination time. When the trip is over, the Chronocar will appear at whatever location on Earth I choose."

"That's amazing." Ollie was wide-eyed.

"Well, it's not quite perfect. I was off by about 10 feet when I got here. That's why there is a big hole in your ceiling."

"So, you can go anywhere in time that you want?"

"Almost. You can't go to the future, because it does not exist. So, I can only go forward to about the time when I left. I can't go beyond that."

"So, are you going home now?" Ollie said.

"I was planning on going back tomorrow."

"Will you ever come back?"

"You know I will!"

"Oh." Her expression softened. "I, uh, was just hoping you wouldn't go away mad. Because of Daddy, I mean."

Tony shut down the computer. "I still think he's wrong, but I guess it won't hurt to be more careful when we're out and about. I do want to see a little more of 1919 before I go. We just won't talk to anybody or anything, I promise. So, will you show me around?"

"Daddy's asleep in his chair in the front room," she said with a grin. "We could go out for a while and get back before he wakes up."

Tony smiled mischievously. "Let's do it."

Ollie and Tony climbed out of the Chronocar. "Put on your new suit and give me a little time to get cleaned up," Ollie whispered as she picked up the bucket of water.

A few minutes later they tiptoed past the doctor, who was quietly snoring in his chair, and stepped outside. It was still very warm out, so Tony decided to forgo the jacket and tie. Ollie took Tony's arm as they strolled down Vincennes Street; then they turned west on 47th Street.

"Where are we going?" Tony asked.

"Oh, I thought we'd go to White City."

"White City?"

"An amusement park. You know, rides, sideshows, and games."

"Colored people going to a place called 'White City'?" Tony grinned. "Just seems a little odd."

Ollie laughed. "You don't understand, honey. They named it White City after the Columbian Exposition. They moved a lot of the things there from the fair."

Tony felt a tingle when she called him "honey."

"Is it walking distance?"

"No, we're going to take the elevated."

It was all strangely familiar as they climbed the stairs to the 47th Street station, Ollie lifting the hem of her long skirt as she stepped. He had been on these steps and at this station many times in the future, where there was a lot of concrete and steel, and things were brightly lit. Now, though, the station was made of wood, and it was dimly lit but clean. She gave the agent two nickels, and they pushed their way, one at a time, through the turnstile. After a wait of about 10 minutes the train rattled down the track. It looked like an ancient version of the rapid transit Tony used to ride—heavier, clunker, and probably sturdier—in spite of the fact that the cars also appeared to be made of wood.

The light inside the car was faint, given off by clear, naked electric bulbs that dimmed when the motor engaged. Ollie sat by the open window on the hard leather seat and held Tony's arm tightly while a gentle wind played through her hair. It was a noisy ride, so they spent most of the time looking out the window at the city below, the darkness broken up by solitary lights on the street corners.

At the 53rd Street stop, a number of people got on the train. One young, fair-skinned black woman headed toward them.

"Hey, Ollie!"

70

Ollie looked up. "Hey, Susie," she said, pulling away from Tony. "How are you doing?"

"I'm doin' okay, girl. Who is this?" Susie took a seat in front of them.

"This is Tony. He's visiting from Africa."

"Africa? Really?" Susie peered at Tony.

"Yes, ma'am." Tony was getting tired of faking the accent.

"Where you goin'?" Susie asked.

"I'm taking him to White City."

"That sounds like fun! I'm going to see my momma," Susie said.

"And how she doing?"

"She okay." Susie sighed. After a minute of silence, she added, "Ain't it sad about Mickey?"

"Mickey? Walgreen's Mickey?" Ollie frowned. Susie nodded. "What about Mickey?"

"You don't know? They say he dead, girl!"

"What?" Ollie said in a shaky voice. "What do you mean?"

"They was some colored people in the store today, and some white men wanted to get 'em. Mickey and Mr. Jamison protected 'em and got 'em out. But the white boys was so mad they killed Mickey and Mr. Jamison! Beat 'em both to death! Then they burned the place down."

"Mickey? Not Mickey!" Ollie's lips quivered, and she began to sob.

"Killed them?" Tony said to himself, forgetting his accent. "Could that be my fault?"

"What you mean, 'your fault'?" Susie asked.

"That was us!" Ollie cried. "Mickey died trying to save us!" Tears ran down her cheeks.

That wasn't supposed to happen, Tony thought. Could Dr. Johnson have been right? Would Mickey and Jamison dying change history significantly? It still didn't make sense. Maybe they would have died anyway. Yes, that was it. The troublemakers would have come to the store whether he and Ollie had been there or not. Still, Tony could not help feeling responsible. Sure, there were other black people in the store, and Mickey and Jamison would have tried to help them. But Mickey had helped Tony and Ollie escape. How much time had passed between their escape and the attack on Mickey and Jamison? A lump formed in his throat.

"Oh, I'm so sorry, Ollie. I know Mickey was a good friend," Susie said.

"Ollie," Tony said calmly. "This is our stop. Come on."

"I'm so sorry, honey," Susie said softly.

"It's okay," Tony said as he coaxed Ollie out of her seat. "Let's go.

You'll feel better."

Tony could see the park from the platform. There were dozens of ornate whitewashed buildings, all outlined in a number of dazzling lights. He could make out a Ferris wheel and three crude-looking rollercoasters. A tall illuminated alabaster tower with a bright rotating searchlight stood in the middle of it all. Ollie smiled weakly as they made their way down the stairs. The entrance stood on the northwest corner with a huge, ornate square-shaped structure with bare light bulbs arranged to spell "White City" along the top.

They stopped at the gate, and Ollie bought two tickets at 10 cents each. They entered the park.

"What's first?" Tony asked.

Ollie shrugged sullenly.

Tony stopped and took her by the shoulders. "Look, Ollie, I feel terrible about Mickey, too."

"I just had to have that Coca Cola," Ollie said.

"It's not your fault."

"It is!"

"No, it is not! It's not your fault those racist bastards killed him." Ollie wiped the tears from her eyes. "Mickey was very brave to help us," Tony said, taking her into his arms as she whimpered. "Blame the men who killed him, not yourself."

"But if we had not gone there…"

"It is not our fault," Tony said. He explained how he thought the bad guys would have come anyway, and Mickey and Jamison would have tried to protect anyone who was in the store. They would have beaten them and burned down the store whether he and Ollie had been there or not.

Ollie dried her eyes with a frilly kerchief. "Some white people are so hateful. Kill their own kind if they try to help a colored person. We just live in an evil, hateful time. You're right; they would have killed poor Mickey anyways." She stuffed the kerchief back into the pocket of her skirt. "I just hate that we were there when it happened. That we couldn't have done something to prevent it."

"What could we have done? We had no idea that was going to happen. Why don't we try to enjoy ourselves a little, okay?"

Ollie smiled halfheartedly. "All right," she said softly. "Take me down the boardwalk."

They strolled along the wooden walkway and admired the large artificial lake on their right and fancy, luminous buildings on the left. Tony had many questions about the rides and attractions. There was a tiny town that was home to a group of little people, or "midgets," as she called them, and sideshows with fire-eaters and sword-swallowers. Little shops and stands sold curious trinkets and snack foods like Eskimo pies and Oreo cookies. They came upon a building with a huge and rather disturbing red thing on top—a big demon with bat wings. Ollie explained that it was a funhouse. Tony had no idea such things existed this long ago.

"Oh, Tony, let's get a tintype!"

"A what?"

"A tintype, you know, a photograph of you and me."

Ollie grabbed his hand and led him to a large whitewashed wooden booth with a sign that advertised tintype photographs for 75 cents.

They stepped into the dimly lit booth just as another couple was walking out. Tony was taken aback by the pale, blonde-haired young woman who gave them an evil look as they passed. It was difficult for him to get used to the fact that there were people here who hated him simply because he was black.

"Hello. You two want your picture made?" The proprietor, dressed in a full suit, tipped his straw hat at Ollie as he invited them in. "You want something formal, or would you like a novelty?" He gestured toward some large boards with cartoonish drawings of circus clowns and convicts in striped uniforms, with holes cut out where the faces would be.

"Um, just a regular picture, please," Tony said.

"Just have a seat there, and I'll be right back." The man stepped into a back room.

Ollie sat in the ornate wooden armchair with plush green cushions in front of the image of a fancy parlor painted on the wall. Tony stood behind her and whispered in her ear, "Where I come from, we call this a selfie."

"A what?" Ollie giggled. He held his phone up and snapped the picture.

Tony quickly put the phone away when the man came back in carrying what looked like a black leather envelope. The camera was a big wooden box on a tripod with a lens in front. The man removed the photographic plate from the leather envelope, opened the back of the camera, and set the plate inside. Then he walked over and had Ollie place her hands in her lap and adjusted her hat. He had Tony stand just behind the chair and instructed him to hold his head high. "Don't you move, now!" he said as he stepped back behind the camera. He picked up a flash lamp, a T-shaped device with a long wooden handle and a narrow trough at the top, which he filled with a white powder. "Okay, don't move, and don't let the flash scare you, now! You ready?"

"Yes, we are," Tony said through his teeth.

The photographer removed the cover from the lens. "One, two, three, four, and five!" He pulled a handle on the flash lamp, and there was a loud pop and sizzle as the flash powder ignited, lighting the room with a brilliant white for a couple of seconds. He placed the cover back on the lens and waved away the smoke. "That's it, all done. You can come back for your photo in about 15 minutes."

"That was interesting." Tony grinned. As they exited the booth they were greeted by a loud splash to their right. What looked like a barge full of people had just hit the water in the little faux lake after barreling down some sort of incline.

"Oh, Tony! Let's Shoot the Chutes!"

Ollie nearly dragged him to the entrance of the ride, where they rode a tall escalator with wooden steps to the top. After a brief wait in line they climbed into one of the boats and sat next to a white couple, which made Tony a little nervous until he realized that they didn't seem to care. *How do you know whom to trust and whom not to trust?* he thought. Next thing he knew they were sliding down the ramp at breakneck speed. They all yelled giddily with their hands in the air. They passed under a bridge and hit the water with a splash that nearly drenched them all. The boat rocked wildly in the water, though Tony could swear the pilot of the boat was rocking it even more.

"Wasn't that fun?" Ollie giggled as she wiped the spray from her face. "Let's go get our picture and ride the Observation Wheel next!"

Their clothes dried quickly in the warm air as they made their way back to the tintype booth. Tony wondered what the photo was going to look like. The man handed him a small brown paper envelope while Ollie paid him. Tony removed a thin metal plate about the size of a playing card. The tintype had a surprisingly sharp image of Ollie sitting regally in the chair, while he stood behind her with a strained smile.

"This is amazing." He stared at the picture while they strolled down the boardwalk. He was impressed by the quality that was possible in this time.

The Observation Wheel was the gigantic Ferris wheel, bigger than any he had ever seen. The riders sat in metal boxes with wooden seats that could hold six people. They stood in line with white couples in front of and behind them. Tony would bristle when a young white man or woman would look at them with a scowl. Skin color just seemed to be an awfully random reason to hate someone whom you didn't even know. Yes, there were racial problems in 2015, where it seemed like almost weekly there was some kind of racially fueled violence reported in the news. He still did not understand it, since he had never experienced any of it himself. He attended IIT, a school with a student body made up of young people of all races and creeds from all over the world, and there had never been a problem that he was aware of. So, all of this irrational hatred was still alien to him.

For the most part, though, the white kids on the Ferris Wheel were just there to have a good time, just like Ollie and Tony. Or so it seemed. When their turn came, none of the whites wanted to ride with them, so Tony and Ollie had a car to themselves.

It took a few minutes of starts and stops to load everyone on. Then came the exhilaration of the ride through the air, up to where they could see the nighttime city, and then down, whizzing past the people below. Ollie seemed to have forgotten about Mickey for the moment. She held on tight to Tony, squeezing him a little as they reached the zenith. For a moment they seemed to float in the sky. The breeze was cool, and the sweet sounds of music and laughter filled the air. The scent of hot dogs and popcorn grew stronger as they coasted down and faded as they circled back up. Ollie laid her head on his shoulder and looked at him with big, moist eyes. Tony gave her a quick peck on the lips. She blinked in surprise and smiled. He leaned in to kiss her again.

The car rocked as the ride abruptly stopped. They were nearly at the top. It seemed too soon for it to be over. Tony sat up and looked around. The sounds from below had changed. Instead of laughter, there were shouts and screams. A large crowd had gathered a few hundred feet away, and groups of people gathered in a few places around the park. He could clearly see men fighting.

"What the hell is going on?" he whispered.

"Oh, Lord, I should have known."

"Known what?" Tony asked.

"Something must have happened. Coloreds and whites are fighting each another. That's why poor Mickey got killed. Something bad happened someplace, and now there's gonna be trouble."

The ride jerked forward and eased to a stop after a few seconds. Tony looked down and saw they were letting people off, but no one was getting on. Policemen, who reminded him of old Keystone Kops of the silent movies, were breaking up fights. He wondered how fairly the justice was being meted out.

When they reached the bottom, the old white man who operated the ride opened the gate and let them out. "Park's closed. Ya better get while the gettin's good!"

Soon they were walking briskly down the boardwalk, arm in arm, moving through the crowd. "So much stuff going on between whites and colored people this summer," Ollie said. "I guess sooner or later…"

"Hey! You goddamn niggers still here?"

Tony glared at the pimply-faced teen yelling from a crowd a few yards away.

"I'm talkin' to you, boy! Get the hell outta here!" he called in a pubescent screech.

Fear and anger welled up in Tony's gut. The punk was not alone. There were four others with him, and as he yelled, more white faces turned their way, some laughing, some scowling. Tony had many white friends. In fact, he never even thought of his friends in terms of black, white, or anything else. It was strange to look upon white people now as the potential enemy. He glanced at Ollie, who was trembling. There were no black people anywhere. Were there ever any in the park in the first place? All he knew was that he and Ollie were now totally on their own. It was the cover of night, and the chaos allowed them to get by without being noticed by too many people. Most of the patrons were only interested in getting out of the park away from the trouble.

Lots of people, white people, were gathered just outside the gate. Some were standing around a couple of defiant black teenage boys who refused to be bullied. The shouts attracted more young white men who gathered around to join the fun.

"They're gonna kill those poor boys!" Ollie cried.

"Come on," Tony said as he took her hand. Taking advantage of the distraction, they walked out of the gate as fast as they could. They got to the corner and started for the train until he realized that the elevated platform could easily turn out to be a trap if some thugs decided to make heroes of themselves.

"Is there another way home?" Tony said quietly.

"The trolley, a block this way," Ollie said.

"Just keep walking." Tony glanced over his shoulder. Lots of commotion, but no one was following. They reached a trolley stop, and he started to calm a bit as they stood alone. For several minutes they waited and said nothing.

"Ollie," he felt obliged to explain, "I'm sorry, but…"

"No, don't apologize. I just don't know how white people can be so hateful. I'll bet you don't have this problem in your time."

Tony tried to explain how some racial strife was still apparent in his time. But in his isolated suburban existence, whites, blacks, and everyone else just seemed to get along. Many of the families in Park Forest were even interracial. There had been some protests and even riots triggered by racially charged events in his time that he had seen on the news. But he had never been an actual victim of racism. Until now. He finally understood the fear and frustration his predecessors had had to deal with over the centuries.

Dr. Johnson's warnings were ringing in his ears as Tony tried to figure out how to get Ollie home safely. The big red streetcar finally came banging down the street, its bell clanging loudly. Ollie offered a feeble smile as he helped her aboard. There were a few people on the trolley, mostly black and a few whites, who sat in the front. *Guess they don't know about the trouble,* he thought.

They took seats near the back and rode quietly. Ollie said they would have to transfer once to get back home. He glanced at her as she leaned on his shoulder, staring out the window with a look of anger and dejection that bordered on tears. He put his arm around her and squeezed a little. She responded by moving closer.

"Tony," Ollie said quietly. "Couldn't we just go back in time with your Chronocar and warn Mickey? Maybe we can prevent him from getting killed."

Tony mulled this over. It did make a certain amount of sense. But what if they did? Would it be the right thing to do? Perhaps Mickey was supposed to die. What would be the consequences of keeping him alive?

"Hey, feller!" the conductor called from the front. "Hey!"

Tony looked up, surprised to see that all of the other passengers were gone.

"You better get off here!"

Tony bristled. "What are you talking about?"

"Take it easy!" the conductor said. "Better come up there and take a look for yourself."

Tony walked to the front of the car. There was a crowd of a dozen or so white men about two blocks ahead standing on the tracks.

"When I came through here about an hour ago, them fellers took a colored man off and beat him up something awful," the conductor explained. "I don't want no part of that. You and yer lady friend better get off now. They might not see ya from here."

Tony thanked him as he and Ollie got off at the rear of the trolley car. They waited for it to start down the street, then quickly walked in the opposite direction. Tony glanced back and saw the men swarm the trolley car, but no one came their way.

Ollie shivered. He held her hand tightly, wondering if she could tell that he was shaking, too. He looked back several times to make sure they were not being followed. When they got to the corner and turned, he relaxed a bit, and they slowed their pace. Tony peeked around the corner of each building before they crossed a street or an alley. He kept a watchful eye in all directions, prepared to run if he detected a threat. If what Ollie said was true, they would not be safe until they got back to her house, but not even that was a guarantee. He held her hand tighter.

He wanted to stop, hold her, and comfort her, but he dared not ease his vigilance or breathe a word out loud lest someone hear them. Ollie whispered that they were on the outskirts of a white neighborhood. Tony figured they had made it this far only because the people here did not know whatever it was that was going on. Most people would not know what happened until they read it in the papers the next day. It was a little risky, but it was the quickest way home.

They walked for 15 minutes without incident. Even the occasional white person sitting on a porch or looking out of a window did nothing more than stare.

"You all right?" Tony asked softly.

Ollie nodded quickly. "I guess you can't wait to get back home," she sighed.

A crazy thought went through his mind. A stupid idea. "Why don't you come back with me?" he blurted. "Just for a visit. You could spend a week in 2015 and only be gone from here for an hour."

Ollie looked at him, her eyes glistening in the soft streetlights, and smiled. They walked along, gazing at each other, as they started across a street.

"Hey, you! Nigger!"

Tony's heart seized. He peered down the street behind him. Five white men were coming their way. Tony cursed himself for his carelessness.

"I'm talkin' to you, nigger boy!" The voice echoed among the buildings.

He gripped Ollie's hand. "Run! Now!" He led her down the street, hoping to lose the men before they got to the next corner. There were distant footsteps as the men gave chase.

"Wait a minute! It's the girl we want to talk to!" one of them bellowed as the others laughed.

Ollie grabbed the hem of her skirt and held it as she ran. Tony pulled her along as he desperately looked for a doorway, an alley, or any means of hiding or escape. He glanced back and saw the men turn the corner. He prayed for a policeman, wondering if a cop would help or simply join in on the fun. Tony's heart pounded as he heard the footsteps get closer. They were going to catch up with them. He had to do something—protect Ollie, at least, and not just because of how he felt about her. He also had to consider the fact that had it not been for him, Ollie would very likely not be out tonight, and that Dr. Johnson was right after all. Any harm that came to her and the subsequent changes in history, however subtle, would be his fault. The bizarre events of the last two days flashed through his mind—the encounters and the tragedy that might never have happened if he had not gone out with Ollie, if he had never come to 1919.

He decided to turn the next corner and then urge Ollie to run on ahead to save herself. Using the element of surprise and his limited fighting skills, he might be able to keep them occupied long enough for Ollie to get away. Yes, that was what he would do. He just hoped Ollie would follow his instructions and not try to help him fight.

"Ollie, listen to me!"

Bang!

Ollie went limp. He tried to hold her up, but she fell clumsily to the ground and rolled onto her back, pulling him down with her. He got up onto one knee, lifted her head gently, and felt the warm oozing from the back of her neck. Her eyes were closed, but she was still breathing.

The men had gathered in front of him. Tony looked up at their pale faces in the gloomy light. Some were grinning, others looked astonished; one little guy seemed to be scared.

"What the hell you do that for?" one of them said.

"I was trying to shoot him, not the girl. It was a mistake!"

"Come on, finish the job, and let's get outta here."

This was it, Tony decided. He wasn't going to give up without a fight. He tightened every muscle in his body. He'd go for the one with the gun first, and then he would try to get as many of them as he could before they killed him. Who knew? Maybe he would get lucky.

"Hey! That's Ollie!"

Tony was shaken by the familiar voice. A large figure pushed through the group—Bobby McNab.

"You son of a bitch! You shot Ollie!" McNab turned on the man with the gun and threw him to the ground, his huge hands closing around his neck. "You goddamn son of a bitch!" McNab was banging the kid's head on the sidewalk.

Tony looked around frantically. *The gun! Where's the gun?* By the time he spotted it on the ground, one of the other men had grabbed it and pressed it to McNab's temple.

"You crazy? Get up! Let him go!" the gunman growled.

McNab slowly rose to his feet. He turned to Tony and then looked down at Ollie's motionless body lying in a growing pool of blood. "Ollie, I...I didn't know it was you! I'm so sorry!" McNab looked Tony in the eye, tears streaming down his flushed cheeks. "I'm so sorry! I didn't know! I loved her. I would never hurt her. I loved her!"

"You goddamned nigger lover!" one of the punks growled. McNab was on him in an instant, bloodying his nose with one punch. It took all four men to restrain him.

There was the shrill of a whistle, and the men froze.

"What's goin' on over there?"

Tony turned and saw two policemen running their way.

"Shit!" one of the men spat as he threw the gun into some nearby bushes. "Come on!"

McNab stood there staring at Ollie when one of the thugs seized him by the collar.

"Stupid fool! Let's go!" the man said as he pulled McNab.

McNab backed away. "I'm so sorry," he mouthed to Tony, and then he turned and scurried away with the others. The policemen arrived seconds later—one white, and, much to Tony's surprise, one black.

"You better go on after them while I look after these two," the black cop said. The young white officer nodded in agreement and ran after the gang.

"Call a paramedic!" Tony cried.

The policeman gave him a strange look as he knelt down and put his ear to Ollie's chest.

"Call a doctor or something. Come on!" Tony screamed.

The officer sighed and placed a hand on Tony's shoulder. "It's too late for that, son," he whispered. "It's too late for that."

Chapter 10

7:40 a.m.

The rising sun was soon hidden by gray clouds that covered the city with a cooling curtain of showers. The raindrops thumped lightly on the leather top and streaked down the windshield of Dr. Johnson's automobile as he drove home from the city morgue with Tony in the seat next to him. Whenever Tony tried to speak, the doctor frowned and put a finger to his lips. Tony was more than a little surprised at Dr. Johnson's demeanor. He had just lost his only daughter to a violent crime, and the perpetrators would not only get away with it, but they would likely be celebrated for it. There had been some tears earlier when the doctor had to identify Ollie's bloody, broken body, but now he seemed strangely calm. Presently the rain slackened, and the orange sun peeked between the clouds, casting surrealistic, elongated shadows along the glistening sidewalks. Tony waited until they were inside the house to speak.

"Dr. Johnson, I…"

"Tony, here is what I want you to do." The doctor looked very focused as he took him by the arm and sat him on the couch in the parlor. "You said you asked Ollie to go out with you last night, right?" He took a seat next to Tony.

"Well, yes, but…"

"So, it was your fault. I mean, if you had not been there—here—she never would have left the house, right?"

"Probably not, but…"

"Hear me out. You're the reason Ollie is dead. It happened because you were here and because you did not heed my warnings."

Tony stood up. "Dr. Johnson, how could I have known that…?"

"Sit down, son," he said calmly. "I'm not blaming you. I'm sure you never would have done anything to hurt her. You told me yourself how you tried to protect her."

Tony eased back onto the couch. Pangs of guilt ran up and down his spine. He knew it was his ignorance, stubbornness, and his unwillingness to listen to the doctor's reasoning that resulted in Ollie's brutal death.

"But it was your fault. You do see that, don't you?" the doctor said.

"Yes, but I have an idea."

Dr. Johnson shook his head. "Listen. You are going to take the Chronocar and go back a few hours before the time you went to White City. Only this time you will make sure Ollie doesn't leave the house. I know it's dangerous, perhaps more dangerous than either of us may realize, but I am convinced that Ollie was not supposed to die. At least not now. That bullet killed her and any children, grandchildren, and great-grandchildren she might have had. Tony, you have to do this."

"Yes, Dr. Johnson. I had exactly the same idea." Tony let out a heavy sigh. "I should have listened to you. You have no idea how terrible I feel. The only thing that has kept me going these past few hours is knowing that I can fix this. And I will. I'll start reprogramming the computer."

"Don't leave until we get a newspaper. We'll need to know everything we can to make sure that we—that you—don't somehow interfere with history some other way."

"Okay," Tony said, "but I'd better go back at least three days."

"Three days? Why?"

"I have to go back to before I first arrived on Saturday. I don't want to meet up with myself!"

———————

Tony labored over the keyboard. It only took a few minutes to set up the parameters for the 72-hour trip. He saved the data and ran a simulation. It looked good, as if it should work with a comfortable margin for error. To be safe, he ran it again. This time the outcome was different. The first simulation showed he would transpose a few miles above the Earth and reappear a few minutes later in the same spot in Dr. Johnson's house. The second simulation had the Chronocar materializing several feet below the ground. The input was exactly the same.

"Is everything okay?" Dr. Johnson poked his head inside the time machine.

"Almost." Tony explained the computer error that could result in the Chronocar materializing halfway between the first floor and the basement.

"You will have to take that chance," the doctor said.

Tony grumbled. He wished he had gotten a more powerful computer. When he examined the output, the error was minuscule. Traveling over great temporal distances was relatively easy. The little PC could easily monitor the systems and make corrections if needed. The trick was not to travel faster than the computer could make the calculations. Short trips—and this one would only take about 20 or 30 seconds—was another story. He decided to run several simulations and average out the results.

"Is there any way I can help?" the doctor said as he stepped inside.

"Sure. You can check behind me and make sure I am entering the information correctly."

Tony began running the simulations and recording the data. "You never told me about your PhD degree," he said as he stabbed the keyboard. "There can't be too many black men with that level of education in this time."

The doctor told Tony how he'd gotten a PhD in physics and mechanics from Tuskegee, a rather dubious degree since Tuskegee was a school of applied science and did not teach physics. He went on to explain how his discovery of the tattered, old copy of the *Principia* had instilled a desire to learn more, and when he'd heard there was a school for black men, he'd saved up his money to go to Tuskegee to further his education. It wasn't until he actually got there and met Booker T. Washington and Dr. George Washington Carver that he learned the disappointing truth about the school.

Tony stopped typing and turned to the doctor. "Seriously? Booker T. Washington and George Washington Carver were two of the most famous black men in history."

"Great men who went out of their way to help a fellow colored man, a poor son of a slave." He spoke of how the two men told him they could not provide the knowledge he sought. They recognized his genius and offered him a chance to get a free education and work at the school, but he was not interested in agriculture or animal husbandry. As it turned out, Washington and Carver were black men of great influence, their achievements recognized by many white scholars. They were able to convince some white colleagues from Cornell University to provide books, lessons, and exams and evaluate his work. After four years of long-distance learning, while also working as an assistant to Carver, he had achieved the equivalent of a PhD, but there was no way Cornell would give him such a degree. So, Washington and Carver awarded him a PhD in physics from Tuskegee, knowing that essentially it would be worthless; it was the only way they could acknowledge his achievement.

"You completed the equivalent of an undergraduate, graduate, and doctorate degree in four years?" Tony said, stunned.

"Yes, it took a long time."

"Takes most people twice as long."

Dr. Johnson shrugged. "It seemed a long time to me."

Tony had run the simulation 15 times, averaging the results. The worse that might happen would be materialization six inches above or below ground level. They both decided that he would have to live with that. Dr. Johnson stepped out of the Chronocar as Tony prepared for the trip. Several minutes later he stepped out of the time machine as Dr. Johnson entered the room.

"Here's the paper." The doctor handed him the copy of the *Chicago Herald Examiner*. The headline screamed about some little girl named Janet who had been murdered. There was a picture of a little, light-haired, white child. The riots were mentioned in a smaller sub-headline.

4 DEAD, 50 INJURED IN RACE RIOTS

Clash between Whites and Negroes at 29th Street Beach Spread throughout the City.

The newspaper reported that two young Negro boys swimming just off the beach had been throwing rocks at a young white man, who threw rocks back at them, hitting one in the head. The boy drowned. When a fight broke out, it infected the entire city. It had been a hot, racially tense summer. Sooner or later something would have triggered the violence. Later in the article there was a list of the dead and injured. Two of the dead were identified as a young white man named Mickey O'Grady who was killed by a "mob of Negroes," and a Negro woman, Olivia Johnson, who had been shot after she and her boyfriend started a fight with some white youths and tried to run away.

"That's not what happened," Tony said to himself.

"Certainly not. How could the two boys have thrown rocks while they were swimming?"

"No, I mean Ollie and me… That's not the way it happened."

"The *Defender* won't be out for a couple of days yet. That's where the truth will be," the doctor said.

"I don't understand any of this," Tony said with frustration in his voice. "I did my homework. I went through the books on Chicago history. I Googled the year 1919 and went through dozens of websites. I looked through all of the old newspapers. I probably read this issue of the paper! There was nothing about any of this. None of this violence was supposed to happen until sometime in August. I mean, I would not have come at this time if I'd known there was going to be trouble."

"Could you have done something, maybe something small and seemingly insignificant, that might have somehow led to this?"

Tony shook his head. "I told you what we did. I had that run-in with McNab at his shop, and he wasn't even mad by the time we left. There were lots of black people in the drugstore. The guys who killed Mickey probably would have done it anyway. They didn't come back until hours after we were gone. My being there couldn't have made any difference."

Dr. Johnson stroked his forehead. "All I know is that Ollie should not have been there. She should not have died. And you have to fix that. Are you ready?"

"Looks like all I have to do is keep Ollie at home."

"Good." He gave Tony a piece of paper with writing on it. "When you see me, show me this, and you will have my unquestioned cooperation."

Tony read the note, clumsily pronouncing the words, "*Tempus neminem manet?*"

"It's Latin. It means 'Time waits for no one.' Please remember it. If you say this to me, I will know you are a time traveler and that I should trust and listen to you. Best be on your way, son."

Tony started for the Chronocar. He paused and turned back to the doctor. "What will happen to you here once I leave?"

Dr. Johnson stared at Tony for a moment. "Good luck, son," he said, "and please be very, very careful." He walked out of the room. A moment later Tony heard the front door open and close.

The Chronocar seemed to be in good operating condition. He had been a little concerned that some of the mechanisms might have been damaged in the fall, but it now seemed that a few nonessential switches and lights had been the only casualties. The seat harness was still damaged, but he did not have time to fix that. He figured that when zero gravity kicked in, he would just hold himself down for what should be a very brief trip.

Through the window he watched the room dissolve away. But instead of the blackness of space he had anticipated, he saw an almost-white brightness that astonished him, then he plummeted into a stomach-wrenching free-fall. He had transposed only a few miles above the Earth, still within the atmosphere and the grasp of gravity.

He fell, spinning wildly, through clouds, then through clear sky, so fast that he could not tell how close he was to the ground. It was all he could do to keep himself in his seat. Through the vertigo he was able to focus on the monitor screen. Numbers blurred past as the little computer tried to keep up with the constantly changing coordinates. He hoped he would be out of transposition before he hit the ground.

The Chronocar stopped falling and spinning even more suddenly than it started. The only thing not tied down inside was Tony, and he was flung to the top of the sphere, then to the floor, with a force that nearly rendered him unconscious. It took several seconds to clear his head.

Chapter 11

Tony climbed out and looked around. He was in Dr. Johnson's house but not in the parlor where the time machine had landed before. The Chronocar was now in the dining room where Dr. Johnson often sat in his chair to read the newspaper and take naps. He walked into the parlor and saw that the hole the sphere had created in the ceiling the first time was not there now. Clearly, this was a time before his first arrival.

Outside he heard a muffled crash, followed by howls and shouts. Without thinking, he darted out the front door. A crowd of black people was gathered in a circle in the street. There were more cries as people hovered closer. Tony pushed his way through the group. A man, or what was left of a man, lay crushed on the cobblestones. Splinters of wood and bits of torn fabric were strewn about him. "What happened?" he asked.

A man standing next to him spoke without looking up. "Didn't you see it? He fell out the sky! He just fell out the goddamned sky!"

"Oh, my God!" Tony gasped. He rushed back inside and scrambled into the time machine. When the Chronocar materialized in the living room, it landed on the exact spot where the doctor's chair sat. The doctor, who must have been sitting in his chair, was transposed to where the Chronocar had been seconds earlier, half a mile above the earth in free-fall. He tried to imagine what it might have been like to be calmly reading a newspaper one moment, then falling through the air. He probably passed out or died of a heart attack before he hit the ground, Tony hoped.

He needed to go back just a few hours and arrive in the middle of the night. That way, if he materialized anywhere other than a bedroom, everyone should be safe. It was going to be tricky. He wouldn't have much time before the people outside figured out that it was Dr. Johnson who was dead in the street and come to the door. He opted not to test the new parameters on the simulator and began the countdown for the transposition sequence.

Through the Chronocar's window he could see Ollie rushing to the front door. She opened it, and several agitated people were trying to push their way in. One man saw the Chronocar and froze. They all turned to look. Just as the room began to fade away, Tony heard Ollie scream.

What a damned mess! He braced himself as the Chronocar fell and spun wildly. This trip would last a little more than eight seconds, and he prayed the computer would perform at least as well as before.

Chapter 12

This time he was ready when the Chronocar stopped, holding on to the seat and console tightly. He was in the parlor again, almost in the center of the room. It was early morning, the light of the rising sun streaming through the window. Tony cautiously exited the time machine and noticed that the bottom of the Chronocar was embedded a couple of inches into the floor.

There were heavy footsteps on the stairs. Dr. Johnson entered the room holding a baseball bat, with Ollie hiding behind him, both in bathrobes. Dr. Johnson's jaw dropped, and he put the bat down.

"*Tempus neminem manet*," Tony read slowly from the note.

The doctor was wide-eyed as he took the note from Tony.

"That's your handwriting!" Ollie said. "But what does it mean?"

"It means we need to listen to everything this young man has to say."

Tony suggested they all sit down as he tried to explain everything that had happened. When he got to the part about the trip to White City, he gazed at Ollie and hesitated. The doctor gave him an understanding nod and asked Ollie to go make some breakfast. Tony showed him the newspaper with the story of the riot that was going to start in three days, and Ollie's terse obituary.

"What I plan to do is make sure everything works out okay. Make sure Ollie doesn't go anywhere, that she stays safe. Then I'm going home," he said.

"I see," the doctor said. "Well, you seem to be dressed appropriately enough. Tell you what…after breakfast, I'll take you on a little tour. A controlled tour. It's the least I can do for the man who saved—who is *going* to save—my daughter."

"Thank you, sir."

"Just promise me that you will do what I say and not talk to anyone."

"I have definitely learned my lesson," Tony responded.

They went to the kitchen and sat at the table, where Ollie set steaming plates of scrambled eggs, bacon, and hominy grits before them. She poured each of them a tall glass of cold honey lemonade. Tony dove into the food, being extra careful with the bacon.

Chapter 13

Friday, July 25, 1919

8:30 a.m.

Tony sat in the front seat, while Ollie sat in the back of the doctor's almost-new 1918 Oldsmobile. They could have ridden convertible-style, but Dr. Johnson had the leather roof on to keep the hot sun off their heads. The only glass was the windshield, which had an upper section that could flip up. The hard leather seats were a lot like the ones on the elevated train and the trolley—not at all comfortable. The wooden dashboard was flat and only had a few dials and switches. The steering wheel rose up from the floor where there were three pedals, the accelerator and the brake, but Tony could not guess what the third pedal was for. The engine was noisy, and the ride over the cobblestone street was bumpy. Tony enjoyed every moment of it. They turned west from Vincennes Street, and after a couple of blocks, they turned right onto a major thoroughfare.

Tony was trying to figure out what Ollie thought about him. She was friendly but not as warm or as interested in him as she had been the last time. It was the same person but at a different time. She really seemed to like him before. He wondered if she would develop an interest in him later and if whatever it was that they had before was inevitable. Could three days make that much of a difference?

"So, Tony," Ollie called from the back. "Recognize anything? Anything that might be an old relic in your time?"

"Actually, this street looks very familiar." He frowned as he looked around. "That's it! A good friend of mine will live in that building 90 years from now. We're on King Drive."

"This is South Parkway," the doctor said flatly.

"Oh, right! That's what it was called before they changed the name. In the late '60s, they renamed it King Drive after Dr. Martin Luther King, Jr." Tony could not recall if he had mentioned King before. Then he realized it would have been during his previous visit, two days from now. "Martin Luther King was a minister who led the civil rights struggle. He did a lot to fight racism in America."

"I'll bet he is loved and respected by everyone," Ollie said.

"Actually, he was assassinated."

"Really? When did this happen?" the doctor asked.

"Before I was born. 1968, I think."

"How old was he when he died?" the doctor said.

"He wasn't very old. Maybe 40 years old, I think."

"Are you certain?"

"Yeah. There were riots in the streets and stuff when it happened. Why do you ask?"

"Just curious," Dr. Johnson said.

"You know, in my time," Tony changed the subject, "they call this area Bronzeville."

The doctor frowned. "Will they build a foundry here?"

"No, sir," Tony said. "Bronzeville—bronze as in bronze skin. This area, from about 22nd Street down to 60-something, is going to become a major and important black, uh, colored community. It will become a little famous, actually."

"Wait. Past 55th Street?" the doctor said. "Surely colored people won't take over Hyde Park!"

"Well, they won't 'take it over,' but it will be a very integrated neighborhood. All kinds of people will live there. Mostly because of the University of Chicago, I guess."

"Colored men attending the University of Chicago?" Ollie was agape. "That's unbelievable."

"Colored women, too," Tony informed her.

"Really?" Ollie said.

Tony could not identify many of the streets they drove down until they approached the lakefront from Indiana Boulevard. "Oh, my God," he gasped. He recognized a couple of buildings, but what really struck him was how few buildings there were. There were a few elegant structures on Michigan Avenue but almost nothing next to or behind them. Grant Park was there, but all of the trees were small and young. They drove down Michigan and turned onto Washington Street.

"There's the El," Tony chuckled.

Ollie smiled. "You got elevated trains, too?"

Tony turned in his seat to look at her. "Yes, and it's the same one. Newer trains, but the same elevated tracks." As they drove under the tracks, he added, "The stations look similar, too."

When they got to State Street, he was astonished to see the traffic and congestion. Cars, trucks, trolleys, horse-drawn wagons, and the choking stench of exhaust fumes and horse excrement. They inched over to the curb, and Ollie got out. She trotted around to give her father a kiss on the cheek, then she smiled and waved to Tony as she went into the alley next to Marshall Field's.

"There's certainly a lot of traffic," Tony commented as the doctor maneuvered the car back onto the street.

"Used to be worse," he grinned, "back when there were more horses than cars."

They made their way through the confusion and turned north onto State Street. Trolley cars moseyed up and down the middle of the road, and automobiles crept behind the occasional horse and carriage. Policemen tried in vain to regulate the traffic at the intersection, but it was a hopeless, unbelievable mess. As they inched down the street, Tony noticed that there was no Chicago Theatre. When they finally made it to Wacker Drive, the doctor turned right.

"I'm trying to remember if the Wrigley Building or Tribune Tower would be visible or if they would even have been built yet," Tony said as he scanned the skyline to the north.

"The what?"

"Guess not." Tony grinned. "They're going to be built just across the Michigan Avenue Bridge on the other side of the river."

"There is no bridge," the doctor said as they drove past where the bridge should have been. "Michigan ends here. That's Pine Street there on the other side of the river. Just some factories and warehouses. I've heard talk about building a bridge and improving that part of town, but that would probably be a long time from now."

"When I come back," Tony said absent-mindedly, "I'll bring you some pictures. You won't believe how much all of this is going to change in a few years."

They drove south on Michigan Avenue. The only building on the east side was the Art Institute, complete with the patina-encrusted lions standing guard. Everything looked a lot cleaner and brighter than in all the old black-and-white historical photos. The doctor pointed out a few notable buildings here and there while Tony observed what would be there a century later. When they reached 35th Street, Tony asked him to turn right. They passed under the El again, and they took another right at State Street.

"Okay, it's gotta be here somewhere."

"What are you looking for?" Dr. Johnson asked.

"There it is! Turn left here!"

They drove down the little tree-lined street and stopped across the street from a big, red stone building.

"The Armour Institute?" the doctor said, puzzled.

"This is my school. In a few years, it will become Illinois Institute of Technology. I'm supposed to graduate from here in 2016. Do you mind if I got out and looked around?"

"That would not be a good idea in this neighborhood," the doctor said. He shut off the engine. "We can sit here for a minute or two, I guess."

Tony pointed out that in his time the campus stretched south to 35th, north to 31st, and east to Michigan. The big Armour building would still be there and so would Machinery Hall, the squat garage-like building they were parked alongside. Another huge red brick building stood where the Galvin Library would be, and to the west he only saw a quiet tree-lined street, no Dan Ryan Expressway.

"You never told me what happened after you got your PhD from Tuskegee," Tony said.

Dr. Johnson looked a little surprised. "I don't remember telling you that."

"We talked the last time I was here a couple of days from now."

Dr. Johnson chuckled. "I see." He told Tony the story of how he left Tuskegee and came to Chicago where he had been told the opportunities were better. He found there wasn't much call for a black physicist anywhere. He'd tried to get a job as a professor or even a high school teacher. The white schools laughed at him, and the black schools did not know what to do with him. None of them recognized a physics degree from Tuskegee. He ended up getting a job as a butcher, which he did for years. That was when he met Ollie's mother, Martha. They got married, had Ollie a couple of years later, and lived happily for a while. Then Martha died of consumption when Ollie was 10 years old. He caught it, too, but it only left him a little weakened. So, he pretty much raised Ollie alone.

"Now, may I ask you something?" the doctor said.

"Of course."

"Have you ever read *Frankenstein* by Mary Shelly?"

Tony was startled at the question. "I saw the movie," he said, wondering what an old horror classic had to do with anything.

"Then you might remember how the Frankenstein character suffered in that story. See, he created something he hoped would be a great scientific boon to mankind. Instead his creation was an abomination, a murderous monster. And as long as the beast lived, Frankenstein suffered a wretched life, feeling responsible for the death and suffering of innocent people."

Dr. Johnson sighed. "I had hoped that my theory of time travel would be a wonderful scientific discovery—the kind of thing that would probably never

93

really happen but that could lead to other discoveries. I mean, when I wrote that paper, I figured there was no way anyone could ever make anything like a mechanical brain controller."

"You mean, like my computer?" Tony asked.

"Yes." He rubbed his eyes. "Time travel is a very dangerous thing, Tony. The most innocent thing you do here could change the future in the most serious way."

"And what about the part of your theory that says the timeline is fixed? That 2015 still exists as long as I exist? And that I should not be able to change anything significantly?" Tony asked.

"I was wrong. The timeline was fixed as long as you were inside the Tesla field. Once you turned it off, you became part of this time, and what you do can and will change history."

"I wish I had understood that before. So, I'll do what you say. I'll avoid people and make sure I don't interact with anyone. I'll just stay with you and Ollie until I know she is safe, and then I'll go back home."

The doctor sighed. "There is a lot more to it than that. Son, I created a Pandora's Box, and you unwittingly opened it. I have changed the world. No, I have changed the universe. What I have done could mean the end of the world—of everything as we know it. Everything!"

"You're not making any sense."

"Tony, you said you found the *Negro Journal of Science* in the back of a library. What happened to it afterward?"

"It was a reference book. I made copies of your article and left the book there. I had to."

"So, someone else could find it and build a Chronocar. Surely other copies will survive. Who knows how many others are going to see that article, figure out the Tesla thing, and build a time machine. Can you imagine dozens of reckless, irresponsible people gallivanting through time? Imagine the chaos! The history you know may already be a changed history, changed by some clumsy time traveler. How long before some fool does something really stupid that wrecks everything? And when that happens, it will be my fault!"

Tony turned and looked into his troubled eyes. "Doctor, the ability to go back in time can just as easily be a godsend. Imagine being able to go back in time and preventing Pearl Harbor from happening by warning people first!"

"You are confusing me. What is this about Pearl Harbor?"

"Okay, let's see. It's 1919. World War I just ended, right?"

"World War I?" the doctor gasped. "You mean there will be more world wars?"

"In about 20 or 25 years, I think, the country will be pulled into a war when the Japanese stage a surprise attack on our navy base in Hawaii."

"No!" The doctor covered his ears. "Tell me no more! I don't want to know! This is the thing I feared most!"

"But we could help people!"

Dr. Johnson hung his head. "You say this surprise attack results in a lot of death and destruction. Yes, a terrible thing. But what would happen if that raid does not take place? It's hard to imagine, but preventing that attack could be worse than letting it happen. You say this attack will draw this country into the war. What would happen if we never entered this new world war? Who would win? What would the world be like? How can we possibly know what would be the right thing to do?"

"But using your discovery, we could save lives, prevent wars. Warn people about earthquakes and floods. We could make the world a better place."

"That is the domain of the Almighty! I should not even know these things about the future."

"But how the hell can you knowing that make any difference?"

"Look," the doctor said as he turned in his seat. "I now know there is going to be another world war. Let's say Ollie gets married and has a son. And now my grandson wants to join the army. I will be the only person on this Earth who knows that he would likely end up fighting and possibly dying in a war. So, what do I do, stop him from joining the army? I mean, it is all so complex and intertwined. You have laid an unbelievable burden on me by telling me this. No man should ever know the future!"

Tony sat dumbfounded. He stared at the doctor for several long moments. He wondered how it could not be a good thing to prevent the assassination of good men like King and the Kennedys or the horrors of 9/11. What would his world be like if those things had never happened? How could death and destruction be a good thing?

"You make it sound like I should destroy the Chronocar when I get back, and go find that book with your article and destroy it, too," Tony said.

The doctor seemed to be preoccupied with something across the street. Tony followed his gaze and saw two young white boys pointing at them. "I'm sorry, what were you saying?" Dr. Johnson turned back.

"Do you expect me to go back and destroy the greatest discovery ever made? Sooner or later someone else will find your article or maybe figure it out for themselves."

"I know. I have already tried to find and destroy as many copies of that journal as I could, but there were 150 copies printed and sent all across the country. I could never find them all. Even if you were to destroy your Chronocar and the book you found, the Pandora's Box has already been opened. The monster has been let loose…" The doctor's voice trailed off to a whisper. "The end has begun, and there is nothing I can do to stop it."

There was a loud thump in the back of the car. They turned in their seats. The little white boys were throwing rocks at the car. A stone flew through the opening in the back and nicked the doctor on the ear.

"Why, those little…" Tony opened the car door.

"No! Tony! I'm okay! Don't!"

Tony was already out of the car, chasing the boys down the street. His plan was to chase them for a block and just scare the hell out of them. The boys disappeared around the corner. Tony stopped and chuckled. He had turned and started walking back to the car when he heard a voice behind him yell, "That's him! That's the one!" He peeked over his shoulder and saw the two boys standing next to a couple of hefty-looking young white men.

Tony started running back toward the car. The two white men gave chase.

"Hey! Get back here, nigger!"

Tony ran full speed, but he could hear them catching up. He thanked God when he saw exhaust coming from the tailpipe of Dr. Johnson's car. He literally dove into the backseat, and Dr. Johnson stomped on the gas.

Tony sat up in the backseat, breathing heavily.

"This is not going to work," Dr. Johnson shouted over the noise of the engine. "This is not 2015, son. You are going to have to watch yourself!"

"I just wanted to scare them!"

"Well, those big college boys were going to do more than just scare you. Have you forgotten what I just told you? You are now part of this time. You can be hurt. You can be killed. What then? You have to promise me to be careful and control yourself."

As they drove off in silence, an image of Ollie's lifeless body lying on the sidewalk flashed through his mind. Could Dr. Johnson be right? He decided that he would watch himself, be very careful. He'd hang around for the next three days to make sure no harm came to Ollie, and then he would go back home. Then he would have to decide what to do about the Chronocar.

Chapter 14

Friday, July 25, 1919

2:15 p.m.

Jonathan Weeks was livid. Never in his 58 years had anything so utterly outrageous ever happened to him or his family. And what was he going to do about it? What could he do about it? He leaned on his cane as he hobbled into McGinty's Pub and plopped down on a stool.

"A pint!" he growled to McGinty behind the bar.

"What's wrong with you, Weeks?" Seamus Shaughnessy sat on the stool next to him.

"What ya think? I'm so fuckin' mad, I could kill the filthy…"

"Whoa!" Seamus said. "Calm yourself. What's the matter? Is it Danny again?"

"What do you mean by that?"

"Last time you came in here this hot, your grandson Danny was in some kind of trouble," Seamus said as he picked up his mug and took a sip of ale. "Did he do something again? I mean, the little guy can be a real troublemaker."

Seamus ducked just in time to avoid Weeks's backhand.

"There will be none of that!" McGinty shouted. "Ya want your pint or not?"

"Give it here," Weeks growled.

"You settle down now, Johnny. No fightin' in my place."

"Sorry, Johnny," Seamus chuckled. "I didn't mean to get yer dander up."

"Well, it is about little Danny, but not what you're thinkin'."

"So, what has got you so riled?"

Weeks downed the cool pint of ale in one swallow. He wiped his mouth with his sleeve and slammed the mug on the counter. "Another," he yelled. "Me grandboy Danny," he turned back to Seamus, "he was a-walkin' down the street with his little friend Sean. Just mindin' their own business over by the Armour Institute, when all of a sudden, this goddamn nigger starts chasin' 'em. No reason. Probably just wanted to beat on some poor little white boys. Scared the livin' shit out of 'em. By the time he got home he was starting to have one of his fits, you know?"

"Yeah, one of them seizures, you mean," Seamus clarified.

"Yeah, that." Weeks downed half of his second mug. "Anyways, he and

97

his little friend are runnin' for their lives. They turn the corner and run into a couple of big college boys."

"This happened over near the Armour place?"

"Yeah. When the college boys saw the nigger chasin' 'em…well, they started chasin' that filthy nigger."

"They catch him?" Seamus grinned. "Beat the black off of him, did they?"

"No, the lousy bastard had a buddy with a car. Before the college boys could catch up with him he jumped in the car, and they drove off."

"I can see why you're so mad."

"Wish I could get my hands on that nigger," Weeks fumed as he finished his drink. "Kill 'em, I would."

"Like the niggers who damned near killed you?" Seamus grinned.

"Don't get him started on that again," McGinty groaned.

"Who tried to kill you?" a young, dark-haired man said as he walked up to the bar and stood behind Weeks.

"Who the bloody hell is this?" Weeks looked the young man up and down.

"This here's Archie Hogan, a new member of the club."

"Who tried to kill you?" Hogan said with an intense expression.

"Lousy niggers robbed me and threw me off a train." Weeks slammed the glass down on the bar.

"Hey, careful with that!" McGinty took the empty mug from him. "That was over 30 years ago, man. Get over it."

"Get over it! You expect me to get over this?" He banged the cane on the bar. "I been a damn-near cripple ever since, and it's gettin' worse."

"Give him another beer, on me," Hogan said. "So, how did this happen, Johnny?"

"Oh, Lord, here we go again," McGinty said as he filled the mug.

"I was asleep in a boxcar on me way to Alabama. When I woke up, I caught these two niggers going through me pockets. When I tried to fight 'em off, the big one picked me up like a sack of potatoes and threw me off. Threw me off a movin' train, he did!"

"You'll never find the nigger who was chasin' your Danny," Seamus said. "Wouldn't know if you had the right one, anyway. They all damn well look alike."

"Hell, I'd be happy to give it to any nigger," Hogan said.

"So, let's do that. Why don't we get the boys together and go get us some niggers." Seamus smiled. "Have a little fun."

"Aye." Weeks's eyes narrowed, and his mouth turned up to an evil grin. "Let's stop by my place first."

Chapter 15

Friday, July 25, 1919

6:50 p.m.

Tony and Ollie were on the front porch enjoying the cooling temperatures. Ollie sat in a rocking chair, while Tony leaned against the railing. They watched people stroll up and down the sidewalk as the occasional car or horse-drawn wagon passed by.

"So, tell me about the future." Ollie smiled.

"Here, I'll show you." Tony took his smartphone out of his pocket.

"Hey, Ollie Baby!" A tall, lanky man wearing jeans and a dirty T-shirt came strolling across the street.

"Damn!" Tony whispered to himself.

Ollie sighed. "Jojo! Don't you come over here!"

Tony quickly put the phone away as Jojo walked up to Ollie. "Aw, baby!" he pleaded. "I jus' wanna talk to ya."

"I don't want to talk to you," Ollie sneered.

"Ollie, sweetheart!" Jojo grinned, showing all of the teeth he still had. "Why you do me like that?"

"She said she doesn't want to talk to you," Tony said, hoping this time he could bluff Jojo away.

"Who is this nigga?" Jojo scowled at Tony.

"This is Tony," she explained. "He's my, uh, cousin from St. Louis."

"Well, then, Tony from St. Louis, why don't you mind the hell your own business?" Jojo walked up to Tony who instinctively backed away. "That's right, that's right," Jojo said as he pushed Tony up against the wall. "You know what to do. You ain't nothin'!"

Tony's body shook as the anger and fear welled up in him. If he did anything to hurt Jojo, it could lead to more trouble that he would have to go back and fix. What was more likely would be Jojo hurting him, which wasn't exactly a pleasant thought either.

Tony watched as a third possibility unfolded. Ollie grabbed Jojo by the shoulder, spun him around, and planted a small, tightly balled fist in his face. Droplets of blood flew from his nose. Jojo lost his balance and fell to the ground. As he rolled, something fell from his hand and skidded across the sidewalk.

"My phone! You bastard, you picked my pocket!" Tony grabbed the device off the pavement.

"What you hit me for?" Jojo held his bloody nose. "Damn!"

"I told you not to come over here, Jojo." Ollie stood over him, one hand on her hip, and shook a finger at him. "Now, you just get your skinny self up and get away from here."

Jojo got up slowly. "You didn't have to hit me."

"Go home, Jojo." Ollie turned away.

Jojo walked back to the other side of the street with his hand over his face and his head down. When he reached the far sidewalk, he turned around and said, "Wanna go to the show with me tomorrow night? I'll pay this time."

Ollie fumed. She picked up a stone and threw it. Jojo ducked just in time. He shook his head and walked away.

Tony was befuddled. The encounter with Jojo was eerily similar to before yet not quite the same.

"I went out with that fool one time," Ollie said, rubbing her knuckles. "Now he thinks I'm his girlfriend. He's just too nasty."

"I guess I should thank you."

"I'm sorry, Tony." She smiled. "Daddy said that you have to stay out of trouble. I didn't want you getting into a fight with Jojo. You might have hurt him."

Tony smiled weakly. "You did a pretty good job of that."

<hr />

Later that night Ollie sat next to Tony on the sofa. "Daddy explained what happened. You saved my life...or you are going to save my life. I don't know. I just feel like I should thank you."

"Well, I kind of had to. You were not supposed to die. I mean, I should not have been there in the first place. It was my fault."

"It wasn't your fault. You didn't know that was going to happen. They killed me, and you came back for me."

Tony took her in his arms and held her tight. "It's okay now. You're going to be fine. All we have to do is make sure you don't go out tonight."

Ollie was crying. Tony held her tighter. She wrapped her arms around him. The tears and the embrace were probably just platonic, just simple gratitude, but he could not contain his arousal. Why couldn't she be someone in his time? All the women he knew back home seemed so shallow. In college he experienced the paradox of women who seemed to be interested in him because he was bright but who couldn't care less about him as a person, because they wanted to find a husband who had the potential to be successful and wealthy.

Tony wanted someone who liked him for himself. Someone like Ollie. Her tears subsided as he stroked her shoulder. She looked up at him with big, sad eyes. Lovely eyes. Beseeching eyes. Her full lips quivered. He leaned closer and kissed her. A warm, releasing kiss. A wonderful kiss. A kiss that took a century to happen.

She unwrapped herself from his arms and stood before him. *She's beautiful,* he thought, as he tried to imagine her slim frame under all the clothes. She began unbuttoning her blouse, slowly exposing perfectly shaped breasts.

Tony's eyes were fixed on her. He was a little surprised that she was not wearing a lot more underwear. She dropped the blouse and beckoned him with a finger. She undid the buttons on his shirt, pulled it off, and cast it aside. They embraced and kissed, long and hard. *My God,* Tony thought. *Who would have known that Ollie was so hot!* He could actually feel the heat. Like flames around him. And smoke. He could smell the smoke!

Smoke?

Damn. He had fallen asleep on the cot, fully dressed. It was one hell of a dream, but what had woken him? Smoke—thick, black, choking smoke—hovering at the ceiling. He jumped out of bed and turned toward the stairs. A bright orange flicker was visible under the door. He darted upstairs, choking on the fumes. The kitchen was in flames. The curtains and the icebox were alight. His eyes and lungs burned as he ran through the house and forced himself upstairs to the bedrooms.

"Doctor! Ollie! Wake up! Get up! Fire!" he shouted as he burst into Ollie's room. She was coughing in her sleep. He shook her awake, picked her up, and put her on her feet. "Get outta here, now!"

"Daddy!" Ollie shouted.

"I'll get him. Go on, get out!"

Ollie ran down the stairs, screaming and coughing.

It took a moment for Tony to locate Dr. Johnson in all the smoke. Tony tried to shake him, but he didn't move. He shook harder. "Dr. Johnson! Get up! The house is on fire!" The doctor remained motionless in his bed. "Oh, God!" Tony cried. "You can't be dead!"

Tony jumped when he heard a loud bang downstairs. He stumbled down the steps. The front door was open as smoke poured out. When he got to the door, he saw Ollie in her white nightgown lying face-down on the porch in a pool of blood.

His eyes welled up. "What the…?"

In the street a half-dozen or so white men stood around a car, three with guns in their hands. Behind them flames danced in the other houses across the street.

"There's another one, Johnny!"

Tony jumped back through the door. Bullets followed him.

"Don't let him get away! Go in and get him, Archie!"

"I ain't goin' in there!"

"Burn him out!"

Tony's vision was blurred by tears and smoke. He was mad, scared, frustrated, and confused. What the hell was going on? Going back should have prevented Ollie's death. Now Ollie and the doctor were both dead. Was this his fault? They had not even left the house. They were not supposed to die. He must have caused this somehow, and he had to figure out a way to fix it. What had he done in the last 24 hours?

The window in the parlor shattered as a bottle of burning liquid flew into the room, splattering fire across the floor, the furniture, and onto the Chronocar. The Chronocar was on fire, the black hourglass insignia melting away. He snatched a cloth off a little table by the window and tried to beat out the flames. The tablecloth ignited. He tossed it aside and climbed inside the ship. Something thumped against the time machine as flames licked just outside the Chronocar's window. He had to remind himself that the machine was made of metal and that the gasoline or whatever was in the bottle would just burn off.

He started the computer and was shocked to see flames burning outside even after the Tesla field had engaged and after he had transposed into the thin atmosphere. The Chronocar was burning inside the Tesla field! How was he going to put it out? If it was still burning when he landed, it could just start another fire in the Johnsons' house. Should he try to go put it out? Should he change the programming so he didn't materialize inside the house?

The flames began to diminish and eventually vanished. It had used up all the air outside. Now he just had to deal with spinning and falling through the sky.

Chapter 16

Thursday, July 24, 1919

3:35 p.m.

When the Chronocar materialized this time, it was daylight in Dr. Johnson's parlor. Tony stepped out and looked around. The house appeared to be empty. He went into the kitchen and found a newspaper on the table. If it was today's paper, then he had done it right—at least 24 hours before his last two arrivals. He judged from the angle of the sun outside that it was late afternoon. The doctor and Ollie should be home soon. He decided to sit on the sofa and try to relax. He was so tired, he could barely keep his eyes open...

"Hey!"

Tony woke with a start. Dr. Johnson was standing in the open door glaring at him. "Who the hell are you, and what are you doing in my house?"

"Dr. Johnson!" Tony stood. "Uh, *tempus neminem manet?*"

The doctor's eyes widened. "Where is it?"

"Over there."

"It looks like it's been in a fire," the doctor said.

"I'll tell you all about that. Where is Ollie?" Tony asked.

"How do you know...?" Dr. Johnson frowned. "Of course, you knew her and me from before, or rather from the future. If you're here and I gave you that code, something terrible must have happened."

"Please sit down. I have a lot to tell you."

The doctor sat next to Tony and took a deep breath.

"Is Ollie okay?" Tony asked.

"She is still at work. Is she part of all this?"

"Yes, sir," Tony said. "Please, let me tell you from the beginning."

The doctor nodded, and Tony told him about his previous visits, and how each one was a disaster. The doctor's face was expressionless as he listened and took it all in.

———◦◦◦———

Tony wasn't sure how Ollie took to the news that he was a time traveler. She saw the Chronocar, and she trusted and believed her father completely. It was just a lot for her to take in all at once. As they sat out on the front porch enjoying the cooling temperatures, he tried again to explain everything to her and why he had to avoid getting into any trouble this time. They watched people stroll up and down the sidewalk as the occasional car or horse-drawn

104

wagon passed. Ollie sat in a rocking chair, while Tony rested against the railing.

"Tell me about the future." Ollie smiled.

"Hey, Ollie Baby!"

"Oh, what the hell do you want this time, Jojo?" Tony said without thinking.

"Who the hell this nigga?" Jojo asked as he came across the street. He wore a threadbare T-shirt and jeans. "And how he know my name?"

"Uh, that's my cousin Tony from St. Louis," she said.

"How this joker know my name?" He glared at Tony. "Tony, huh? Come here, Tony!" Jojo stood with his hands on his hips. "Wanna talk to you for a minute."

"I don't want no trouble, man," Tony said.

Jojo walked up the stairs, grabbed Tony by the collar of his shirt, and pulled him to his feet. "I said come here, boy!"

Tony pushed him away. Jojo grabbed him again and got in his face.

"Who you think you is, boy?" Jojo shook him and pushed him back down on the steps.

"Jojo!" Ollie yelled.

Jojo turned just in time for Ollie to punch him in the face.

"Hey," Jojo rubbed his cheek. "I wasn't goin' to hurt him. You didn't have to hit me!"

"G'bye, Jojo, and don't come back."

"I wasn't gonna hurt your sissy cousin," Jojo said as he walked back across the street.

"How did you know his name?" Ollie asked.

"I met him when I was here before," Tony said as he watched Jojo disappear around a corner. "You took care of him then, too."

"He's the sissy. He knows better than to hit me back." Ollie frowned. "Let's go inside. I'll make us some cold lemonade."

Tony stood up and brushed himself off. "Aw, shit! Jojo took my phone!"

"I'm gonna kill that fool," Ollie growled.

"We have to get it back!"

Ollie led Tony south, winding through side streets and alleyways to a rougher part of the neighborhood. It was an incredible contrast to the pleasant community where Ollie lived. Here the streets were filthy and smelly, with children in dirty rags scurrying about. They turned down a street where the back of a huge apartment building stood exposed, facing a vacant lot. It was a labyrinth of wooden porches and stairways, with clothes hanging out to dry, flapping in the summer wind. Much to his dismay Ollie led him up one of the rickety stairways, passing people who were trying to catch a breeze sitting among the junk that collected on the porches.

At the third floor Ollie knocked on a door. A middle-aged woman wearing a dingy dress answered. Tony could see at least three little kids playing in squalor inside.

"Ollie, honey, how you doin'?"

"I'm okay, Miss Wilson. We're looking for Jojo. Is he home?"

"Lord have mercy, I ain't seen that boy for almost two days. Spend all his time in the streets. I tell him he need to settle down, get a job, and stay out of trouble…"

"Yes, ma'am," Ollie interrupted. "Do you know where we can find him?"

"He somewhere out there. I don't know, child. He somewhere."

"Okay, thank you, Miss Wilson."

"You welcome," she said, as Ollie and Tony started back down the steps. "You see him, tell him to come on home! I need him to go get my medicine."

They walked up and down the streets, occasionally stopping to ask someone if they had seen Jojo, but he was nowhere to be found. After about an hour they gave up and headed back. Tony cursed himself for being so careless. He wondered if he should just get in the Chronocar and go back again, but he couldn't leave without his smartphone.

"Jojo will turn up," Ollie said, "probably tomorrow."

"I'm sorry, Ollie. That was stupid of me to let him pick my pocket like that."

"It's all right." Ollie smiled at him. "Jojo is not all that smart. He'll never figure that thing out."

"Think so?"

"Yeah. Come on. I am ready for some cold lemonade." Once inside Ollie began cutting and squeezing lemons while Tony sat at the kitchen table and watched.

"In my time no one makes lemonade like that." He grinned.

"No?" She poured a couple of dollops of rich honey into the mixture.

"It comes already made in a bottle. Or you can get a powdered mix that you can add water to."

She stopped stirring the liquid in the metal pitcher. "Why?"

Tony shrugged. "To save time."

"Only takes a few minutes to do it this way." She poured lemonade into two big glasses. "Does it taste better that way?" Ollie said as she set the glasses on the table and sat across from him.

Tony took a deep, long drink. "This is fantastic. The powdered stuff doesn't even come close to this. I don't think they even use real lemon juice."

Ollie shook her head. "I don't understand your future. And tell me something else—where did you get those clothes? Do people dress the same way, too?"

"No, we got this suit at Bobby McNab's. You paid for it."

Ollie looked dumbfounded.

"Uh, I guess you wouldn't remember; it hasn't happened yet. You helped me get a suit at Bobby McNab's so people wouldn't stare and laugh at my future clothes. I mean, I still have my red gym shoes."

"This whole time-traveling thing really confuses me." Ollie scowled at him. "You said I was killed…"

"Twice."

She frowned a little. "So, what happened to me?"

"You were shot both times, and you died."

She sighed. "If you went back in time again right now, what would happen to me? Right now?"

"Um, good question. Nothing, I think." Tony took a sip of his lemonade. "I don't really know."

"None of this makes any sense. How can you be here? How can I die and still be here?"

"Like I told you before, it hasn't happened yet."

Ollie grew silent as her eyes welled up. "Then I am going to die? Sometime over the next three or four days?"

Tony got up and placed his hands on her shoulders. "I came back to make sure you were not going to die." He turned her in the chair and looked deep in her lovely, frightened eyes. "Both times it was my fault. Because I was here, and I was careless. You were not supposed to die. All I have to do is keep you safe for the next few days. Then I go home, and everything will be fine."

Ollie cried quietly.

"When I get back to 2015, I'll check all the old newspapers and public records. If something bad happens to you, I'll come back and fix it."

Ollie wiped her eyes and forced a little smile. "You would do that for me?"

"Of course I would."

Thump! Thump! Thump!

"Who's banging on the door like that?" Ollie stood, wiping her eyes. "Your father?"

"No, he would use his key." She and Tony went to the front door. "What

107

are you doing here?" Ollie said as Jojo pushed himself inside.

"Okay, where the hell is he?" Jojo spotted Tony as he entered the room. "Hey! Just who the hell is you?"

"What are you doing here, Jojo?" Ollie yelled.

Jojo shoved her aside. "I asked you a question, man!" He stomped over to Tony.

Ollie grabbed Jojo by the collar from behind. "Let go of me, woman!" he yelled. He lifted a hand to strike her, but Tony stepped forward and grabbed his arm.

"What's wrong with you?" Tony snapped.

Jojo pushed Tony away. He reached into his pocket and pulled out the smartphone. "Where you get this from, huh? Who is you? What is you?"

Tony reached for it, but Jojo pulled it away.

"Yeah, I figured it out. This some kind of crazy camera thing. There are pictures of Ollie in this thing." Jojo swiped his finger across the screen, going through the various photos. "Where the hell is you from? You...you from the *moon* or somethin'?"

Tony looked at Ollie, who stood agape behind Jojo. "Dammit!" Tony said. "I gotta go fix this."

Jojo grabbed him by the arm. "Hey, I'm talkin' to you. Is you from one of them planets or what?"

"I'm from the future!" Tony shouted. He pulled away from him and stormed into the parlor with Jojo following close behind.

"Oh, my God!" Jojo went limp when he saw the Chronocar. "I knew it! I knew it! Where the hell you goin'?"

"Back in time before any of this happened," Tony said as he walked behind the machine. "Before you came along and stole my damned phone from me."

Jojo's face lit up. "I see now. That's why they live so good with a big house and a new car. You work at a damn hat shop, Ollie, and yo' daddy work at the library. Ain't no kind of way you make enough money to live like this."

"You talking crazy, Jojo," Ollie said.

"Naw, this nigga is how you got to be rich. I see now!"

Tony stepped from behind the Chronocar. "What the hell are you talking about?"

"I tell you what I'm talkin' 'bout." Jojo's eyes narrowed. "You gonna take me in that thing, and we goin' to the future. We gonna get all the baseball scores, find out who gonna win the boxing matches, and all that shit. Then we come back and bet on 'em. That's what we gonna do."

"I don't think so," Tony said, and he went back behind the Chronocar. He needed to get out of here before anything else happened. Jojo was right behind him. He grabbed Tony's arm and tried to force his way into the Chronocar, but Tony caught Jojo in the gut with his elbow, and he fell back gasping. "I'm gonna fix this!" Tony called to Ollie as he stepped inside the Chronocar. Before he could latch the door, Jojo pulled it back open and ripped Tony out of the time machine and onto the floor.

"You ain't leavin' without me."

Tony got up, panting. "And if I say no, what are you going to do?" he growled. "You need me to fly it."

Jojo stood speechless for a moment. Then he walked over to Ollie, who was standing in the middle of the room. "You gonna take me back or else."

"Or else what?" Tony was losing patience.

Jojo planted a hard fist in Ollie's face. She let out a yelp and fell to the floor.

"You son of a bitch!" Tony lunged forward as Jojo lifted Ollie up by her arm, pulled a knife from his pocket, and held it to her throat.

"You take me back or I'll kill her."

Tony froze. Was Jojo bluffing? Would he really kill Ollie? Even if he did, Tony could just go back another day, and she would be fine. But would she suffer now?

Suddenly Dr. Johnson walked into the room. "What's going on here? Ollie?"

"You better sit down, old man, and shut the hell up," Jojo warned.

Dr. Johnson's eyes narrowed. He picked up the baseball bat that was near the door and raised it above his head to strike. Jojo let go of Ollie, grabbed the doctor's wrist with one hand, and jabbed him in the belly with the knife. The doctor doubled over, falling hard onto the floor, and lay motionless.

Ollie screamed.

Tony needed to act fast. He snatched the smartphone off the floor, ran to the back of the Chronocar, jumped in, and latched the door shut. Pain wrenched in his gut as he glanced out of the Chronocar's window and saw the doctor lying in a pool of blood, Ollie standing over him screaming, and Jojo coming his way. He wanted to beat the hell out of Jojo, but he needed to go back in time; that was the only way to fix this.

He powered up the computer as Jojo banged on the door of the time machine. The banging stopped as Jojo fiddled with the door latch.

Tony pressed a key on the keyboard. The Tesla field generator countdown began. *Twenty… nineteen… eighteen…*

The door flung open. "I gotcha!" Jojo yelled as he stuck his head inside.

"Jojo, don't be stupid! Don't come in here!"

"So you can get away without takin' me? You takin' me, nigga."

Eleven... ten... nine... eight....

"Jojo, don't!"

"You scared now, huh?" Jojo began pulling himself in.

"No!"

Three... two... one... Tesla field engaged.

Jojo's expression changed from triumph to terror. A second later he fell inside the Chronocar. Not all of him. The Tesla field had sliced his body cleanly in two. His top half was on the floor of the Chronocar, quivering and oozing blood. The bottom half of his body slid off the outside of the field.

Tony's heart pounded. *What the hell? What now?* He looked into Jojo's wide-open, horrified eyes. They blinked. He was still alive.

Tears formed in Tony's eyes. "You stupid son of a bitch, I tried to stop you." Tony switched off the stasis field and stepped over Jojo's torso. From the outside he grabbed his arms and dragged the now-lifeless carcass out of the Chronocar. Blood spilled onto the floor. He turned when he heard a barely audible whimper.

Ollie was sitting next to her father's body, hugging herself tightly, her eyes as big as saucers, trembling.

Tony walked over to her, tracking blood across the floor. He knelt down and put an arm around her. "I'm going to fix this. I promise."

"He...he...cut half in two!" she squeaked as she pointed to what was left of Jojo. "Half in two."

The doctor lay lifeless as blood puddled under his body. Tony knew he had to be dead. What a damn mess! He let go of Ollie and saw he had smeared Jojo's blood all over her white blouse. She looked down at the red stain and screamed loud and hard.

Tony dashed past Jojo's carcass, almost slipping in a pool of blood on the floor, and climbed into the Chronocar. He sealed himself in and started the computer. Through the window he saw Ollie silently screaming herself into insanity.

A minute later the Chronocar was speeding toward the past.

Chapter 17

There was no one at home. Tony stepped out of the Chronocar into the parlor and peered through the window. The street looked eerily quiet and peaceful. Just then, a black car with spoke wheels and bug-eye headlights pulled up in front of the house, and Dr. Johnson stepped out.

"Dr. Johnson," Tony said as the front door opened.

The doctor stopped in his tracks. "Who are you, and what are you doing in my house?"

"*Tempus neminem manet.*"

"What?"

"*Tempus neminem manet,*" Tony repeated.

"Oh, my Lord!" Dr. Johnson closed the door behind him and stared at Tony for a moment. He looked around and saw the Chronocar in the parlor, its bulk nearly filling the room. He stumbled and Tony rushed to his side.

"No," the doctor held up his hand, "I'm fine. I just need to sit down." The doctor made his way over to his chair. "You know my code. That must mean you spoke with me sometime in the future and felt the need to come back in time, because something went wrong. I see your clothes are covered in blood. Are you hurt?"

"It's not my blood. It's Jojo's."

"Jojo Wilson?" the doctor asked.

"Yes, Ollie's friend Jojo. He tried to hijack my Chronocar…"

"I don't understand."

"He tried to force me to take him with me. Anyway, he got caught in the Tesla field, what you called the temporal stasis field."

"I see," the doctor winced. "Tell me more."

Tony pulled up a chair and told him the whole story, going back to finding the *Negro Journal of Science* in the Hill Library and building the time machine. He recalled the first trip in the Chronocar and saw the shock on the doctor's face when he told of Ollie's death during the race riot.

"That's why I made my first trip back. To keep Ollie from dying."

"You've made more than one trip?"

"Yeah, this is the fifth time I've traveled back to fix things."

The doctor scowled. "Fifth time?"

"Uh-huh," Tony continued. "All told she died twice; you died three times." Tony felt a knot form in his stomach as he saw for the first time the true immensity of the chaos he had caused. "Anyway, I have come back one last time. Once I am sure that you, Ollie, Jojo, and Mickey are okay…"

"Who is Mickey?"

"A white guy who works at the Walgreens on 35th Street."

"You mean the soda jerk?"

"Right. He was killed trying to protect Ollie and me from some white bastards."

"My Lord." The doctor stroked his forehead. "What a disaster! I feared my discovery would be dangerous, but this…"

"I came back to make sure you knew what was coming so you could protect yourself and Ollie. You might not want to be here when those racist bastards…"

"Young man, why don't you get cleaned up and get a little rest? I think I have some clothes you can wear. You have been through a lot. We'll talk more later."

"You're right." Tony sighed. "I'll go take a nap on the cot in the basement," he said, smiling. "Relax, I know where it is."

———◆◇◆———

A couple of hours later Tony put on the clothes that had been left for him—a white polo shirt, blue jeans, and tan deck shoes. He climbed the stairs to find the house empty again. The Chronocar stood where it had landed, with the sooty burn marks on its sides. The ruddy footprints had been cleaned from the hardwood floor. He peeked out the front window. It looked as if nothing had happened. Of course, nothing *had* happened. Yet. The race riot was almost a week away. He spotted Dr. Johnson's car as it pulled up in front. Tony watched as he let himself into the house.

"Doctor?" Tony spoke.

The doctor held up a finger to silence him and walked past him.

Tony went into the kitchen, where Dr. Johnson had started making a pitcher of lemonade. "Where is Ollie?" Tony said.

"She is on a train to St. Louis. She is going to stay with an aunt for a few days. After what you told me, that seemed to be the only way we can be sure she will be safe. Sit down, son."

"Oh, good." Tony sighed in relief as he sat at the kitchen table. Although he was more than a little disappointed that he would not see her again, he was very glad that she was safe. He looked around, remembering how it was when the room was ablaze. "So, do you think I should stay around and make sure that nothing happens to you, Mickey, or Jojo? Or should I just go on back to my time now?"

"What is your time? Where, or rather, when did you come from originally?"

"Two thousand fifteen."

"Really!" the doctor said, stirring the lemonade. "Amazing! Tell me a little about 2015 and how it compares to now."

Tony told the doctor about life in 2015, the modern cars that didn't fly, the racism and poverty that still existed, the diseases that hadn't been cured, and the computer technology that made the Chronocar possible. The doctor was visibly moved when Tony told him of a world made better after the civil rights movement and Dr. Martin Luther King, Jr. and his tragic death. And he was amazed when he heard of the black man who would become president.

"You must show me around your Chronocar," the doctor said as he placed two sweaty, cold glasses of lemonade on the table. He sat down and pushed a glass over to Tony.

"Well, it's quite a mess now with the blood all over the place. Probably all dried now, but I'm sure it's still a little disgusting."

"I see." The doctor took a long drink from his glass. "Tony," he began, "in your visits here, did you ever wonder how it is that I can live so well? I mean, look around you. I have a nice home, an automobile, more than most colored folks—more than many white men, in fact."

"Ollie said you work at the library, and she works at a hat shop. You told me you were once a butcher. I figured you just saved your money."

"I spend time in the library doing research. Mostly trying to locate as many copies of that *Negro Science Journal* as I can and making sure no one else has published anything on time travel. Ollie thinks my 'job' at the library, along with her job at the hat shop, pays for everything. She is a very bright young woman, but I sometimes think she is a little too naïve. Probably my fault. I protect her too much," he said, staring into space.

"Doctor?" Tony said after a moment of silence.

"Sorry," the doctor said. "Tony, you are not the first visitor we've had from the future. Someone else built a Chronocar and came back in time about three years ago. Another young man—a white man—came here from 1998."

Tony gasped.

"Back then we lived in an apartment a few blocks from here, and I still worked in the stockyards. That's when Jason came."

"Who?"

"Jason Sperlinger was his name," the doctor explained. "He was very smart, but his motives were quite different from yours. Jason wanted a lot more than just adventure. He had bigger plans and was diabolically clever. He landed deep in the woods, where no one was likely to find his Chronocar. Jason figured that our apartment would be the only logical safe place for him to stay while in this time. Before making his journey he did extensive research; he figured out where we lived and collected information like baseball scores, horse race results, and stock market prices. He was planning on getting rich, you see…and it would have worked."

"But he would have had the same problem I did with money," Tony interrupted. "I mean, the money from the future looks different, and the dates would have given him away."

"No," the doctor said softly. "Before he left 1998, he bought several ounces of gold. When he got here, he sold it for some of the local currency."

"I see," Tony said, a little embarrassed that he had not thought of that.

"Jason bought some clothes and rented a room from me. You're actually wearing some of the things he brought with him. To Ollie he was just a strange boarder who seemed to enjoy the company of colored people. Not really that uncommon. Jason turned his few dollars into thousands very quickly; in fact, he became extremely wealthy. But that was not the end of his plan. He was going to use the money to buy gold again. Then he was going to go back home with a load of gold, which would have been worth over twelve times as much in his own time. He would have been a multimillionaire. It was so clever. It would have worked."

"What happened to him?"

"He couldn't get back."

"Was there something wrong with his Chronocar?"

"No, he just couldn't get back."

Tony glared at the doctor, not knowing what to make of it all. "Are you saying that I can't go back?"

The doctor stared at his glass and said nothing.

Did he sabotage Jason's Chronocar? Tony jumped up and ran out of the room. If Dr. Johnson did something to his machine, he was going to fix it and go home.

He climbed into the Chronocar, trying his best to ignore the dried blood that was still on the floor. Ollie was alive again, and history was set right—at least as best as he could tell. He so wished that he could see Ollie again, but he could always come back. He would *definitely* come back. Right now, there was nothing more he could do than to get the hell out of there before anything else happened.

He powered up the machine and began the countdown. The Chronocar gave a reassuring hum as the Tesla field generator activated. A loud screech came from below, and the entire sphere began to quake violently. He could feel heat from below and smelled wires burning. Before he could react the entire system shut down. He stared at the computer monitor, looking for some clue as to the cause of the malfunction.

Temporal Transposition Error.

Fail-Safe Engaged.

System Shutdown.

Tony spent several minutes checking the Chronocar's systems. Nothing was wrong, at least nothing that he could see. Now he was angry. Why would Dr. Johnson sabotage the time machine and keep him from going home? He climbed out of the Chronocar and stormed back into the kitchen. The doctor was sitting in the same place, staring into his half-empty glass. Without looking up he gestured for Tony to sit.

Tony fell into the seat. "You knew that was going to happen, didn't you? What did you do to it?"

"I didn't do anything to it." The doctor looked up. His eyes seemed a little moist. "Drink your lemonade and let me finish telling you about Jason."

"Fine, tell me," Tony demanded.

"Jason invited me to see him off. When he started his machine, it reacted the same way. When was the last time your Chronocar behaved that way?"

Tony thought a moment. "Just before I left 2015. My friend Jimmy was helping me test it. It did that when we tried to send it into the future."

"Yes, and why do you think that happened?"

"Because we were trying to send it to a time and place that did not exist. There is no future, only the past and the present."

"You have answered your own question."

"No!" Tony exclaimed. "I came from 2015. It exists. Jason came from 1998, and that exists."

Dr. Johnson sighed. "This is going to be a little hard for you to take, son. Until you got here, 2015 *did* exist. The Tesla field kept you safe, because while you were inside the field, you carried a little of 2015 with you. When you turned the field off, that bit of 2015 was destroyed." He wiped his brow. "Time is an all-or-nothing thing. When you destroyed that little bit of 2015 that you carried with you, you destroyed it all."

Tony shook his head. He didn't understand. He didn't *want* to understand. There had to be a way for him to get back to 2015. There was no way he could be trapped here in the past. Why would time travel be possible if it could only go one way?

"When you came back to 1919 and turned off the field, you brought all of time back with you. You cannot go back to your future, because that future no longer exists now. Don't you see? If this were not true, you would not have been able to save Ollie and me. We are alive now because you erased those days and gave us a chance to relive them."

"But, that means that Jason..."

"Jason brought time back with him, also. Time resumed and worked its way to 2015. Then you brought it back again. However, it seems that whenever time is brought back and restarted, it moves forward in a more chaotic state. Things seem to take a worse turn than before. Let me show you something."

The doctor took some newspapers from a cupboard and dropped one in front of him. "Jason brought this from his time to prove to me that he was a time traveler. Does this agree with history as you know it?"

The paper was dated August 12, 1998. The headline read, "Dr. Martin Luther King Dies of Stroke at 69." Below was a photo of a thin, elderly, white-haired, Caucasian man looking into a coffin from a wheelchair. The caption read, "Among the mourners was former President John F. Kennedy."

Tony's head was spinning. "You mean that Dr. King and President Kennedy were not assassinated in Jason's time? What the hell is going on?"

"Oh, my Lord! This is exactly what I feared." The doctor sighed heavily. "In Jason's first time reality, Dr. King and President Kennedy lived to old age. The world was a relatively peaceful place. From what Jason told us, the civil rights movement was a success almost from the beginning. Negroes and whites learned to live in harmony.

"Then Jason came back in time, and a new time reality began. Things were not as nice. Heroes were murdered. There was more war and crime. Now you are here—again. Haven't you noticed how things got progressively worse each time you went back to fix things? I shudder to think how time will progress forward now."

Tony was dumbfounded as he tried to process what the doctor was saying. All this time he had just been worried about Ollie and Dr. Johnson, while his actions were somehow altering the course of history—affecting everything, everywhere. "Why didn't you tell me this the first time I came back in time?"

"I suppose I might have hoped that I was wrong and that maybe there was a way around it. I don't know. Here, you need to see this."

Under the newspapers were a few typewritten sheets held together with a paper clip. Tony picked it up and read the title on the first page: "The Basic Laws of Temporal Mechanics."

"What is this all about?" he said as he flipped through the pages.

"I have only been able to locate a handful of the copies of the journal with my original article," the doctor explained. "As long as it is out there, I fear that men will continue to build Chronocars and damage time. That is part of another article that I have been working on. It explains the theory of time travel as I understand it now. It also explains the dangers, and I am hoping it will discourage anyone from ever building a time machine. I only hope that I can get someone to publish it. I'm afraid people will find it too fantastic."

"So, if time travel is so dangerous, why didn't you take Jason's Chronocar and go back to stop yourself from writing the article in the first place?"

The doctor sighed. "Believe me, I thought of that. But I could never get Jason's machine to work. Besides, so much temporal energy had already been used that I am really afraid of what might happen if I go back that far. Time is so unstable now, and so many important things have happened since then. If I were to meet up with myself… Well, I cannot imagine what a disaster *that* could be. And like you, I would be stuck in that time—a time I don't belong in. What would I do then?"

Tony tried to make sense of the article, but he was having trouble concentrating. "Doctor, what happened to Jason?"

"I managed to get him back here, and we tried to figure out what had happened. Well, I knew what had happened. It was a part of the theory that I worked out long after the first article was published. Jason had confirmed it. When I finally told him that he could never go home, he got very angry. He wanted to keep going further and further back in time. He wanted to spend his life exploring. He wanted to go all the way back to the beginning! I could not allow that."

Tony's jaw dropped. "You killed him?"

"There was no other way. I couldn't let him go romping around through time." He looked down at his glass and mumbled, "He's buried in the basement."

"But what about me? What are you going to do about me? How are you going to stop me?"

Tears glistened in the doctor's eyes. "I already have."

Tony gazed dizzily at his empty glass.

"You won't feel a thing, son."

Tony tried to stand, but his knees buckled, and he fell to the floor.

117

"H-how could you do this?" Tony asked. He lay on his back, his breathing growing shallow—so shallow that he could no longer speak.

"Believe me, Tony, I didn't want to. I am not a murderer. It was a difficult decision to kill Jason, and it was not an easy thing for me to do. But I had to consider the consequences...

"Then you came along—a bright, young colored boy. I had hoped I could find another way, but you see the chaos that you have left in your wake. God only knows what will become of the world now. I know you didn't mean to do any harm, but everything—all of history—is at stake. I had no choice, son! I had no choice."

Tony could not move. As he stared at the blurred ceiling, memories bubbled up from his evaporating consciousness.

Tempus neminem manet. Time waits for no one.

His first day in kindergarten, when he'd fallen in the mud and ruined his clothes.

Junior high graduation, when he'd proudly graduated on the honor roll.

Tempus neminem manet.

Winning the regional science fair in high school.

Seeing the pride in his father's eyes when they learned he had been accepted into IIT.

Tempus neminem manet.

Finding the *Negro Journal of Science* and building a Chronocar.

The first time he kissed Ollie.

Watching Ollie die. Twice.

Tempus neminem...

Tony's breathing stopped, and his vision faded to black. And for the first time in his life, Tony Carpenter died.

Epilogue

For submission to *The American Standard Journal of Physical and Applied Sciences:*

Dear Editor,

In the August 1901 issue of the now defunct *Negro Journal of Science,* there appeared an article entitled "The Theoretical Possibility of Time Travel." I wrote this article solely as an exercise in astrophysical theory, the culmination of visions and ideas that consumed my thoughts and dreams for many years. In it, I suggested that there might indeed be hitherto unknown energetic forces that govern space and time—that underlying the reality of our universe there is something that quite literally holds all of it together, so essential in function that nothing could exist without it.

From this I extrapolated the design of a ship that could actually harness and influence these forces in such a way that a man could use it to traverse the very seas of time. This fanciful device would require inconceivable technologies to function, such as, for example, a device that I call a "mechanical brain controller," which could make logical, human-like decisions very quickly, tirelessly, and without error. It is difficult now to even imagine the existence of such a mechanism, yet it would be critical in the workings of a time ship. Hence, the whole thing seemed to me to be a practical impossibility.

I submitted this article to several esteemed publications. One responded that they did not deal in science fiction. Others probably did not understand it. In one case, they somehow deduced that the article was written by a Negro and returned it unopened. When I learned of the *Negro Journal of Science,* I submitted, again expecting rejection. As I learned later, this journal would publish almost anything written by a colored man.

I have since come to realize that there is more truth to my musings than I had originally thought, and that the current progression of scientific discovery and practical invention could indeed eventually lead to the mechanisms required to create such a time vessel. For this reason, I feel compelled to share certain facts and theories that I have since worked out and observed. I am also obliged to give a very stern warning to anyone who even dreams of building a time ship based on my first article. There needs to be an understanding of the physics at play, and, more importantly, the calamitous dangers involved.

The following is a simplified version of my Laws of Temporal Mechanics. A more detailed version, with diagrams and formulae, will be forthcoming. However, it has become clear to me that building a time ship could turn out to be a relatively simple undertaking, and I do not want to dissuade those less cognizant of the complexities of physics and mathematics from understanding and heeding the warnings given here.

I appeal to you as fellow men of science to give the following your most serious and sincere consideration.

THE (SIMPLIFIED) BASIC LAWS OF TEMPORAL MECHANICS

I. TEMPORAL ENERGY

There exists an energy that permeates, enables, and stabilizes all of Creation. It is the energy that motivates the passage of time. This "temporal energy," as I shall call it, directs and tempers all other energies, forces, and even matter itself.

Like all other forms of energy, Temporal Energy appears to be obedient to the Laws of Thermodynamics. For example, as the total amount of available Temporal Energy wanes, chaos in the system increases (entropy). Since this energy is gradually being consumed in the natural course of existence, it is reasonable to assume that it will, at some point, become exhausted, resulting in the ultimate chaos—the end of everything. Presumably, and hopefully, this would not occur for eons.

II. TEMPORAL MANIPULATION

Time moves in a specific direction (forward) and at a specific rate (one second per second, sidereal). Newtonian physics states that the application of force can and will affect a change in velocity (speed and direction). Time can, indeed, be affected this way. Time cannot be "traveled," per se. Time is neither a course nor a destination. To "visit" a different point in time is to change the velocity of time itself. Hence, one does not travel through time; one brings the desired time period to himself.

Time manipulation (the changing of its velocity) results in the expenditure of excessive amounts of temporal energy, which cannot be recovered. Therefore, time manipulation necessarily results in significantly less temporal energy being available to the system. Therefore, entropy (chaos) increases.

Time is created with each passing moment. Only the present and the past actually exist. One cannot have access to the future, for it does not yet exist. Time is ephemeral. When time is manipulated and moved to a point in the past, all of the time before that is destroyed. That is, if one moves one year into the past, that year they traveled from (which would now be the future), is no more. It does not and cannot exist.

Time restarts at this point. However, the Temporal Energy consumed in the normal passing of the now-destroyed time and in the manipulation of said time is gone forever. Again, less energy is available to the system; therefore, increased entropy is inescapable. This entropy manifests itself in increased chaos when time resumes. Where there was once peace, there is now war; where there was once economic prosperity, there is now poverty and suffering; where there was once life, there is now death.

To affect the manipulation of time requires a special electrically energized field. I had considerable difficulty working out how such a field could be created and maintained. I shall call it the "Temporal Stasis Field" for reasons I will give below. This field invisibly surrounds the time ship and acts as a time barrier. As time slips by, the man inside is not affected by it. That is, as he maneuvers to the past, neither he nor the ship will get younger. In fact, the space inside the field would contain a bit of the time that he departed from.

If he moved from, say, 1920 to 1910, it would still be 1920 inside the field. These 10 years would still exist and, conceivably, he could even return to his own time. Inside, the time is unchanged, or in stasis, if you will. Hence the name Temporal Stasis Field. However, once the field is turned off, the time that was inside is destroyed, along with any intervening periods. In other words, while the field is on, one could skim back and forth to his heart's desire. Once the field is eliminated, he would be stuck at the destination time, and all time after that would be destroyed. Time would literally restart from that point.

The Temporal Stasis Field is also involved in the actual manipulation of time. It acts as a sort of "propeller" that "rolls" back time. So, it is key to the function of the machine.

III. PHYSICAL TRANSPOSITION

As Dr. Albert Einstein has explained, time and space are connected. What happens in one domain affects the other. Someone traveling a great distance in space at great speeds would experience a dilation of time; he would find himself at a later point in the future than he would anticipate. The reverse is also true. If one "travels" through time, he would experience spatial phenomena. As it "moves back" in time, the time ship would also be transposed in space. It would be illogical for a time machine to remain spatially stationary while moving through time. If you moved a year to the past, the Earth would not be in the same place. Transposition is a natural side effect of time travel. As time is being manipulated, the ship would be transposed to some other point in space, perhaps thousands or even millions of miles away. And, as always, all things are conserved. When the ship is transposed elsewhere, an equal volume is transposed to the point of origin.

A WARNING

As inconceivable as it may seem now, time manipulation is as certain as space travel. The complex and seemingly impossible technologies will one day be easily available. I know this for a fact, because I have been visited by a traveler from the future.

Time manipulation is a detestable aberration of nature that will result in the destruction of time and sap the precious reserve of temporal energy, plunging us all deeper and deeper into chaos. I have been witness to the damage that time manipulation has already done and believe that we now live in a world that is more chaotic than it should be. Are the evils of this world a natural part of our existence, or are they the result of excessive entropy caused by time manipulation?

I believe the latter to be true.

I also believe that this was once a more peaceful and happier world until this traveler came back in time, and, as a result, inadvertently re-started time. Now time has resumed more chaotically, and the evil and suffering that we now experience is evidence of this.

Please do not take these warnings lightly! Although it seems fantastical now, the day shall come when these things will be possible, and the entire world, nay, the entire universe, will be in peril.

Dr. Simmie L. Johnson
September 4, 1919

Biography

Steve Bellinger fell in love with science fiction with the first Tom Swift book that he read as a child. When his mom, who worked for a printing company, brought home an Isaac Asimov novel, he was blown away by it and at the tender age of 13 decided he wanted to write, creating home-made comic books and handwritten manuscripts in wire bound notebooks. As a young adult, he found he just couldn't get his stories published anywhere, so he combined two of his passions, writing and radio, and created several original radio dramas, producing them in his own home-made recording studio.

Through the years he's written content for websites, articles for local newspapers, and even the Junior High Sunday School booklets for the AME Church, but it wasn't until he turned 65 that he realized his dream of having a science fiction novel published, *The Chronocar*.

So, remember, it's never too late!

Steve's affection for science and science fiction continues. He is a lifelong fan of Star Trek (he owns two uniforms) and Dr. Who (yes, he has his own 12-foot long scarf). He's met many of the stars of his favorite programs at conventions, including Nichelle Nichols (Lt. Uhura), James Doohan (Scotty) from the original Star Trek series, and even Tom Baker, the most famous Dr. Who of them all. But the list of celebrities Steve has shaken hands with also includes real-life heroes like NASA space shuttle astronaut Joan Higgenbotham and Buzz Aldrin, the second man to walk on the moon.

Steve lives in the Lincoln Park community in Chicago, Illinois, with his wife, Donna. Find out more about Steve at his website, www.SteveBellinger.com or on Facebook.

Made in the USA
Columbia, SC
03 January 2020